THE SHIMMERING

BOOK 2

The Diary of Gus Childers

MICHAEL L. CLARK

Published by

Historic Traces Publishing

Pensacola, Florida

Paperback ISBN: 979-8-9887856-7-5

Hardback ISBN: 979-8-9887856-8-2

Ebook ISBN: 979-8-9887856-9-9

PROLOGUE

June 21, 1973

As Gus stood at the entrance of the Shimmering, he said goodbye to Daniel, who had become his closest friend. Tears welled up in his eyes as he realized he would likely never see Daniel again. Dressed in his frontier garb of buckskin pants, linen shirt, and slouched hat, he slowly and nervously walked back through the Shimmering.

It took only a moment for him to pass into the new world that awaited him. Gus had not seen his family for forty-six years. He was sixteen years old when he accidentally passed through the Shimmering with his best friend Robbie. He didn't know if his mother and father were still alive.

Summertown, Tennessee, was a long walk from the Gordon House exhibit along the Natchez Trace Parkway. Emily told him he should walk back to the Gordon House and wait for someone to pull into the exhibit's parking lot. There was a public restroom there now, and he could likely catch a ride with someone or ask to use their cell phone.

As he walked south, the weather was beautiful. There was a clear sky, and the temperature was warm - much different from what he had just left. It had been raining all morning. His clothes would dry out pretty quickly now that the sun was shining down on him.

After walking west for about twenty minutes, Gus turned north. Another fifteen or twenty minutes of walking would bring him to the Gordon House. The landscape was nothing like he had expected. He and Daniel had just ridden through this area earlier that morning. It was pretty much an open field when they had come through. Now, it was all wooded. The brush was so thick it was difficult for him to traverse. He got lost more than once because it was difficult to keep his bearings.

After two hours of struggling through the forest, he finally found an open field stretching ahead for about 100 acres. In the distance, Gus saw men and women working in the field. They were hoeing in the dirt, removing weeds from the rows that stretched the entire field's length. Green shoots were growing out of the tilled ground. Gus immediately recognized the two-foot-tall stalks as cotton.

Halfway down on the right side of the field stood what appeared to be an old, dilapidated house. It was a brick structure that had been long uninhabitable. Trees and vines had overtaken the building, winding in and out of the broken windows. Somehow, the house seemed familiar to Gus.

Gus walked to the edge of the field, hoping to stay unseen. He sneaked around the edge of the forest, weaving his way toward the old building. Gus saw that the roof had caved in, and most of the brick from the siding was collapsing and scattered all around. He climbed a mound of bricks and tried to spy inside the old structure. Just as he peeked over the edge of a fallen wall, he heard a voice from behind him.

"Whutcha doin' here, Mista?"

The voice was deep and clear. Gus slowly turned to find a tall, muscular black man standing behind him. The man was shirtless, his pants ragged, and he was barefooted.

Gus nervously replied, "I was just checking out this old house. It looked familiar to me."

The man then said, "You shouldn't be here, Mista. The masta don't much likes havin' people tresspassin'."

Gus asked. "Who is your master?"

"He be Masta Travis Kennedy."

Then Gus said, "Well, this looks like it might have been the old Gordon House. I used to live in this area. Mind if I ask your name?"

"My name is Leroy."

Gus replied, "Nice to meet you, Leroy. My name is Gus. Do you know if this is the old Gordon House?"

Leroy responded, "My grand-pappy told me long time ago, his pappy done worked for the Gordons. That was own more than three-hundred year ago." Leroy quickly looked around to make sure he hadn't been missed.

Gus's eyes widened. Then he asked, "What year is it, now?"

Puzzled, Leroy looked at Gus questioningly. "Don't you know what year it is? Where you been?"

Gus replied, "I've been gone a long time. You might say I've been trapped. I'm trying to get back home."

Leroy then said, "It's 2218."

Gus nearly passed out. His knees buckled, and he fell to the seat of his buckskins onto a pile of brick. Once he was able to gain his composure, he asked, "You said the Kennedys have owned this place for three-hundred years?"

Leroy replied, "Yeah, ever since da war. The Gordons lost it in da war."

Gus asked, "Which war?"

Leroy answered, "Da war between da states, of course."

Gus panicked as he thought about his predicament. When passing through the Shimmering, he had expected to travel from the year 1818 to 2018. It had seemed logical to all involved. Daniel had himself planned to go back to be with his wife, Emily. But instead, Emily traveled through the Shimmering to join Daniel in the year 1818. Why had the Shimmering taken Gus four hundred years into the future instead of two hundred?

Then it came to him. Gus, Daniel, and Emily had all passed through the gateway, traveling south to north, originally. However, this time, Gus moved through, traveling north to south. That must have been the difference. The direction of travel through the Shimmering determined what year you ended up in.

Gus looked up at the sky. The sun was beginning to fade already. "I've got to get back!"

Leroy asked, "Where ya goin', Mista Gus?"

"Sorry, Leroy. I don't have time to explain. I've gotta be somewhere quick!"

Gus scrambled through the brush as quickly as his feet would move. He consistently found himself tangled in honeysuckle vines or briars. He fought them off as soon as possible. Thorns ripped at his hands, causing them to bleed. They slashed his face. On more than one occasion, he prayed, "Oh Lord, help me!"

His head was continually panning the area, searching for the glimmering light of the Shimmering. The sun was now just inches above the tree line. Gus panicked once more when he realized he might not find the portal. He might be stuck here for six months. Maybe even longer.

Finally, there it was. Just to Gus's left, about twenty yards from him. "Praise God!" he cried out as he ran for the gateway. The sunlight was beginning to fade, and so was the portal. With one last burst of speed, Gus flung himself through, diving as if he were jumping into the Duck River's muddy waters. As soon as his body cleared the opening into space and time, the Shimmering closed again. Gus lay face down on the ground, laughing and crying with relief at the same time.

Chapter I

July 12, 1818

The past few months had been like a whirlwind for Emily. She had been so busy planning her scheme to reunite with Daniel after being separated from him for six months.

When she and Ranger Tommy Brown planned to travel through Ittola Chuka, also known as the Shimmering, they had no idea what chaos they would experience. Daniel's friend Jimmy Gleason had been killed going through the Shimmering when he and Daniel accidentally went through in December of 2017. Then, Henry Slater was killed while coming through when he tried to follow Emily and Tommy through back in June. Ilbuk Losa, The Black Hand, killed both men. Ilbuk Losa was a renegade band of Chickasaw who protected the area where Ittola Chuka existed.

As Daniel and Emily reunited, Gus traveled through the Shimmering, trying to make his way back home. Daniel and Emily were suddenly called away to Sheboss Stand, where the Chief of the Chickasaw was ailing from influenza, so Emily could nurse him back to health.

Once Chief William had recovered from his sickness, the Lanes returned to the Gordon farm to determine where they would set up their homestead. But when they arrived, they found the Gordons were under attack by Ilbuk Losa. Daniel and Emily joined the Gordons to fight off the renegades.

Chief William Colbert and his soldiers came to the rescue and turned Ilbuk Losa back to their village. As a gesture of thanks for healing him,

Chief Colbert offered Emily a home in the Water Valley where Beaver Branch and the Duck River meet.

As they all rode down the trail from the Gordon place to Beaver Branch, Emily and Daniel found it difficult to contain their excitement. It took the caravan about four hours to ride from Dolly Gordon's farm to the Water Valley. The trail had not been well-traveled, so it was somewhat difficult for them to make their way through. It was especially tricky for the wagon because the path was narrow. What little travel that had been made down the trail had been done by horseback. Never by wagon. Nevertheless, Emily's mules, Pepper and Rusty, traversed through the tiny trail without much problem.

The sun was already beating down on them when they began at mid-morning. It would be a muggy day. Chief William, along with six of his braves, led the way with Daniel by his side. Jake stayed close to Daniel but would scout ahead from time to time. Daniel seized the opportunity to brush up on his Chickasaw language skills by conversing with the Chief as they rode.

Emily and Tommy Brown came next, driving the wagon pulled by the mules. Two pigs wearing dog halters were leashed to the bottom of the wagon and walked underneath in the shade. Emily's nanny goat, who was now pregnant, was tied to the back, on the right side. Emily's mare, colt, and Daniel's black horse and sorrel were hitched to the wagon's rear on the left side in a string, one behind the other. The rest of the Chickasaw braves held up the back of the caravan.

Emily was filled with excitement as she drove the mules down the trail. She had never experienced this land in such an undeveloped condition. *"Daniel was probably already used to it,"* she thought.

He had been here for several months. But, to her, it was all brand new. The forest around them was teeming with all sorts of wildlife. Birds were singing songs Emily had never heard before. Squirrels chased one another through the treetops. She listened to a trumpeting sound in the distance. "What was that?" she asked Tommy.

"Sounds like an elk," said Tommy. "But I ain't heard one of them in the wild before. Only on National Geographic."

"Wow!" said Emily quietly. "That is so cool!"

After riding for about three hours, the trail began to slope downward. It was a slight grade at first, then about a half-hour later, it was much steeper. Still, it wasn't so steep that the mules had to struggle much. Emily had to apply brakes on the wagon to keep it from rolling up the back of the mules. At that point, Daniel hung back so Emily could catch up with him.

The forest was thinning now. Daniel was waiting in a rock formation on the southeast side of the trail. Daniel said to Emily as she and the wagon approached, "Chief William says this is the border of our land."

Emily looked forward and saw that the trees were opening up into an open valley ahead. Her excitement grew. "How far does it reach?" she asked.

Daniel pointed to a ridge top on the far side of the valley. "To the top of that ridge. I'd say it's about a quarter-mile up past this creek that's coming up. Once we get past the creek, he's going to show us how far up it goes to the north."

Emily smiled and nodded to Daniel in approval. She looked at Tommy, and they glanced at one another in anticipation of what was to come. Tommy was excited but nervous, too. He had left a career with the National Park Service to go with Emily through the Shimmering as her protector. Tommy wasn't sure what the future would hold for him here. He had no way of making a living and didn't know what he would be doing with himself. He just followed Emily wherever she led.

When they reached Beaver Branch, the mules balked momentarily, unsure of the situation. Emily allowed them to take their time, slowly working their way into the water. The branch wasn't broad. It was only about twelve to fifteen feet in most places and only three feet deep at its deepest point. The creek's bottom was lined with silt on top of Tennessee limestone that was flat and slippery. The mules slowly worked their way across without much difficulty. The pigs had to swim at the deepest part of the creek. The nanny brayed as she precariously held her head above the water.

They all gathered and waited until everyone was across as they exited the creek and rode into the open valley. Emily and Tommy stepped down from the wagon and joined Daniel, who had dismounted. The three of them celebrated with hugging and cheering.

"Let's go," said Daniel.

He got back on Hoss while Tommy rode the black. Emily chose to ride the sorrel rather than her mare, Dimples. She left the horse with her colt. They rode up the valley northward alongside the Chief and his braves at a canter.

Daniel tried to measure in his mind as they rode along the bank of Beaver Branch. He figured that they were probably traveling about ten miles per hour at the cadence of their canter. They held their pace pretty well the whole ride.

After about thirty minutes, the valley began to narrow slightly. The ridge on the hillside moved toward the creek. Then, finally, Beaver Branch entered a more significant stream to the east. Jake, who was heavily panting, decided to cool himself in the Beaver. He lay in the edge of the water while lapping it with his tongue. Daniel said, "I think this is Leiper's Creek."

Emily asked, "How long have we been riding?"

Daniel pulled out his pocket watch to check. "About thirty minutes."

Emily smiled excitedly and responded, "So that's what? About a mile?"

Daniel nodded, then said, "A mile long and about a quarter-mile wide. So, it should be right at about two hundred acres."

Chief William approached the group and told Daniel he and his men would ride north. He shook Daniel's hand, nodded to Emily, and said to her, "Thank you." Then he turned his horse and rode away, not waiting for a response.

Chapter 2

They walked their horses back to the wagon to rest them. An hour later, they rode back into their temporary campsite.

"Well, what should we do first?" Emily asked.

Daniel replied, "Let's set up camp first."

The grass within the valley was quite tall. So Daniel found a scythe in the back of the wagon and began cutting the grass in a spot large enough for them to set up their tents. Tommy raked away the grass after Daniel cut it. Eventually, they would need to cut as much as possible so they would have hay to feed the livestock this winter. It was too late in the summer to plant corn.

After they had cleared the camp area, Tommy rode out to find a suitable fallen tree that they could cut into firewood. Daniel and Emily gathered large rocks to create a fire pit for cooking their meals. When Tommy returned, he and Daniel unhitched the mules from the wagon and drove Pepper to where Tommy had selected the log. Daniel drove the mule while Tommy wrapped a chain around the log, and hitched it to Pepper's harness. Daniel drove the mule back to camp, and then he and Tommy used a saw and axes to cut the log into manageable pieces of firewood.

By nightfall, they had managed to unload the wagon, set up their tents, and cook and eat supper. It had been a long day, and they were all exhausted. Daniel said while sitting around the fire, "We need to prioritize things. Emily, what do you think we should do first?"

Emily replied, "I think we need to contain the livestock first. We should build a corral for the horses and mules, pens for the goat and pigs, and a coop for the pullets. After that, I can start planting a fall garden. We also need to get as much hay put up for the winter as we can, and then we can think about building a cabin."

"I agree," said Daniel. "That's a pretty good plan. We'll get started first thing in the morning."

Daniel and Tommy set up a picket line for the horses and mules. They led them down to the creek bank to drink their fill of water, then led them back to the picket and tied them to it for the night. Daniel retrieved a bucket of water for the goat and pigs. He allowed the goat to drink first since she would probably refuse to drink after the pigs. Once she had her fill, he carried the bucket to the pigs, still tied to the wagon's bottom. He set the bucket down in front of them and watched as they stuck their noses in the bucket and blew bubbles through their noses. They drank a little water, then turned the bucket over and started wallowing in the wet soil.

"That figures," said Daniel. "Alright, suit yourselves."

The next morning, they all rose and ate a cold breakfast of jerky and hardtack. Daniel, Emily, and Tommy got started right away with the building. They decided the pigs would be most troublesome to contain, so they started with the pig enclosure. Daniel already had a design in mind. A wooden rail fence could be sufficient for adult pigs if properly built, but the rails would not hold them when piglets came along. Once before, he had problems with piglets crawling through cattle wire to get into his freshly planted field to eat all the seeds. Daniel planned to build a footer or foundation that would make it difficult for the adults to dig under the fence and keep the piglets from crawling under the wall.

First, they staked an area near the back tree line that would still have plenty of grass for the pigs to graze. The pen would be about half an acre, and a large Oak tree rested in the middle of the field that would provide the pigs with lots of shade. Because she was the most capable of driving the mules, Emily would dig the foundation for the fence by digging a trench around the perimeter using a plow. It took her two trips through the boundary to make the trenches deep enough. Tommy and Daniel came behind her, using shovels to empty the channels of any loose dirt.

They needed posts and lumber for the rails and gate, so they all worked together, cutting suitable trees for the job. Cedar would be best for the job, and plenty of cedars were in the valley. First, they built a sled suitable for hauling that they could hitch behind the mules. They cut enough eight-foot posts to cover the perimeter of the pen. Then, they split rails to attach to the posts. Next, they gathered a vast supply of rocks. Stones would be used to fill the trench to keep the pigs from digging under the fence. The rest would be used to build the base of the fence above ground. The rock portion of the wall would stand about a foot tall. They would make mortar for the rock fence out of mud mixed with straw.

It took them seven days to complete the pen, working from sunup until sundown. Once the gate was built and hung in place, they gathered the pigs and the goat and led them by leash to the new enclosure. Eventually, the goat would have a pen of her own. But for now, the nanny could stay with the pigs.

They next began building a corral for the horses and mules. The corral was built just west and north of the pigpen and would be about an acre in size. A small grove of oak trees rested in the middle to provide shade for the animals.

They cut eight-foot posts that would be spaced about eight to ten feet apart. They sank the post two feet into the ground using post-hole diggers that Emily had seen fit to bring with her. Daniel always admired her ability to be prepared for every situation.

They split rails for the cross members. Using a brace and bit, they mortised the posts so that the rails would fit inside. The rails were shaved down on the ends to fit inside the mortise joint of the pole. It was slow and tedious work, but the corral looked just as Daniel had hoped it would once it was finished.

By the end of October, they had finished building a new goat pen and a chicken coop. The next several months were spent cutting logs and dragging them to where they planned to build their cabin. They used drawing knives to strip the trunks of their bark, then stacked them to cure until they were ready to erect the house.

Emily couldn't be more pleased with her mules. It seemed every task they had encountered on their homestead required their use. They were continually hauling or pulling something on the farm that would be too difficult for saddle horses. Emily said to Daniel more than once, "It was the best twelve-thousand dollars I've ever spent."

Chapter 3

December 7, 1818

December mornings in Tennessee are an adventure. One minute, it can be freezing outside; the next minute, it can be sunny and pleasant. That's how this morning started. Around eleven o'clock, Emily was out enjoying the sunshine, doing some laundry. The temperature was still a little chilly, but it didn't seem too bad, with the sun beaming down on her bare arms.

Jake lay on the ground near Emily as she worked. He was soaking up the rays of sunshine as he appeared to be snoozing. Then the dog let out a *"woof."*

He raised his head to look around at something only he heard. He quickly stood and began barking at an approaching rider. The rider rode atop a painted horse while wearing buckskin britches and a buckskin jacket. He wore a fur hat on top of his head. His long raven hair waved in the wind as his horse cantered toward Emily.

Emily was somewhat nervous as the man rode through the Beaver and into her encampment. The man stopped his horse in front of Emily and spoke to her in his own language. Emily held out both hands and shrugged, saying, "I'm sorry. I don't understand." She then turned around and whistled with her ear-piercing tweet to Daniel, who was working down by the corral.

Then, she yelled to Daniel, "Daniel! We have company!"

Daniel walked quickly toward them when he saw the man on horseback. Daniel raised his right hand in a greeting and said, "Hallito!"

The man returned Daniel's greeting and said in Chickasaw, "I am Wind in his Hair. I am friend of David Colbert. He has sent me to find Shobohli Eho. His woman is with child and needs the help of Shobohli Eho. I am here to take her to Sheboss."

Daniel translated what the man had said to Emily. "He's here to escort you. Will you go?"

"Well, of course, I'll go. But I'll need you to go with me. I might need some help."

Daniel called out to Tommy, who was still in the corral. When Tommy arrived, Daniel filled him in on the news. "Would you mind staying here and looking after things?"

Tommy replied, "Naw, I don't mind a bit."

Then Emily instructed Daniel, "Wring out the wet clothes for me while I pack a couple of bags."

Daniel did as she instructed. He pulled wet clothes out of the washtub and wrung the water out. Then, he draped them across the wagon's side to let them dry. Tommy went back to the corral and saddled Hoss and the Sorrel. Emily quickly went inside and packed two saddlebags. She filled one side of her bags with spare clothing and the other with medical supplies. Emily packed Daniel's bags with extra clothing on one side and food on the other side. By the time she had finished and walked outside with the bags, Tommy was walking up with the two horses.

Emily handed Daniel one of the saddlebags, then flung the others over the saddle of the sorrel. She checked the cinch on the horse and asked Tommy, "Did you get it good and tight? You know how he likes to suck wind."

Tommy responded, "I kneed him good in the ribs to make sure. It's good and tight. Don't worry."

Emily then said, "You be careful while we're gone. We won't be gone for more than a week. Take care!"

Tommy replied, "I will. Don't you worry none."

Daniel and Emily mounted their horses, then turned them toward the Beaver while following Wind in his Hair up the trail. Jake followed along, panting with excitement.

After they climbed the hill that led into their valley, they cantered their horses up the trail that led to Dolly Gordon's place. Every thirty minutes or so, they walked the horses to rest them. Within two hours, they found themselves at the junction that turned toward the burial grounds where the Shimmering lay. As they walked their horses, Daniel couldn't help but think about his friend Gus, who had left this world six months ago to return home in 2018. Daniel wondered if he had made it home okay and if he had found his mother and father alive. How would they react to his return after forty-six years of disappearance?

Wind in his Hair began to canter his horse again, so Daniel and Emily picked up the pace to follow him. A ride that generally took about four hours took them just under three. They rode into the Gordon's encampment around three o'clock. Dolly greeted them as they rode up to her house.

"Howdy, Daniel! Emily! Who's your friend?" Dolly asked.

"This is Wind in his Hair. He was sent by David Colbert to fetch Emily. It seems Sarah is having a baby and has requested Emily's help."

Dolly asked, "Do you have time for a bite?"

Emily replied, "Thanks, Dolly. But, no. We've got to get there as quickly as possible. If we could just water the horses, then we'll be on our way."

Dolly replied, "Sure. Help yourselves to whatever you need."

The three riders walked their horses up to the corral, where a watering trough stood. They allowed their horses to drink for a while without letting them have too much. Jake helped himself to the water and scooped it up into his mouth with the bottom of his tongue.

They walked their horses away from the corral and said, "*Thanks!*" to Dolly.

Without mounting, they walked their horses for the half-mile to the ferry that would carry them over the Duck River.

Daniel led the way through the path that led to the ferry. When he came within sight of the barge, he saw that young Tom was no longer working alone. Gus had been the ferry operator for many years for the Gordons. When he left, Tom had to operate it by himself for a while. When he got closer, he realized who was helping Tom. It was Micah Gordon, Dolly's youngest son, who was now sixteen.

Daniel called out, "Hello, Tom! Micah!"

They both responded by waving their hand. When Tom and Micah realized it was Daniel, they both said, "*Hi, Mr. Lane!*"

Then Tom said, "Ya'll needing to cross over?"

Daniel replied, "That we are. Is the fare still the same?"

Tom said, "Two bits per horse and rider."

Daniel handed Tom two coins as he led Hoss onto the barge and said, "Here's two dollars. Y'all can split the change."

The young men both tipped their hats to Emily as she boarded the ferry. When Micah saw the Indian following her onto the barge, he got an uneasy look on his face. Daniel noticed and said, "This is Wind in his Hair. He's a friend."

They all found a suitable place to stand on the barge next to their horses. Jake jumped onto the ferry and began his usual pacing back and forth, looking into the river. "Jake!" Daniel commanded.

Jake walked over to Daniel and stood next to him. "Sit!" Jake obeyed.

Once everyone was set, Tom and Micah began pulling on the ropes to propel the barge across the river. Ten minutes later, they reached the far bank. They all disembarked, then turned and waved at the two young men as they made their way up the trail to Sheboss Place.

They cantered less frequently and for shorter periods now. The trip to Sheboss usually took about six hours, but they managed to make it in just under five. It was already dark when they rode into the clearing where Sarah and David's cabin stood. David met them as they rode up to the cabin.

"Nafkl!" he called out.

Daniel dismounted and greeted David with a hug. "How is Sarah?"

David replied. "She sleeps."

Emily got down from her horse and grabbed her saddlebags. She asked David,

"May I see her?"

David nodded his approval. David then walked over to Wind in his Hair, who had not dismounted. He shook his friend's hand and thanked him for retrieving the Lanes for him. Wind in his Hair acknowledged his thanks, then rode into darkness.

As Emily reached the door, she looked back at Daniel and David and said, "You two stay out of here unless I call for you."

Emily slowly opened the door to the cabin, trying not to make any noise. As she peeked in, Sarah spoke. "Emily? Is that you?"

Emily smiled and responded, "Hey, Sarah. How are you feeling?"

"I'm okay. I get real tired, though. And I'm having these awful pains from time to time."

Emily replied, "That's contractions. How often are they coming?"

Sarah said, "Not often. About every thirty minutes or so. But they seem to get worse every time."

Emily said, "That just means you're getting closer to time to deliver that baby. Mind if I have a look at you?"

"No, I don't mind."

Emily asked, "Are you wearing any bloomers?"

"No, I just got my nightgown on."

"Okay," Emily instructed. "Let's have a look then."

Emily drew back the bedding that was covering Sarah. She then pulled Sarah's gown up, exposing the lower half of her body. Emily then began pushing around on Sarah's belly, feeling the baby within. "Well, the baby hasn't turned yet, but it's still early. Let me see if you've started to dilate yet."

Emily checked Sarah's pelvic area and estimated two centimeters of dilation. "You seem to be doing fine right now. Can I get you anything?"

Sarah asked, "I feel like I need to go to the outhouse. This baby is pushing on my insides pretty hard. Could you grab that bucket for me over there?"

Emily looked around and found a wooden bucket laying in the corner of the room with a lid covering it. She retrieved the bucket and removed the lid before setting the bucket down next to the bed. Sarah hiked up her nightgown and then began to squat over the bucket. Emily grabbed her by her right arm to help steady her as Sarah lowered her body to the bucket. After Sarah had finished urinating, Emily helped her stand up and put the lid back on the bucket. Sarah got back into bed, and Emily helped her settle in for the night.

The next morning, Emily walked out of her cabin room and across the dogtrot from Sarah's room. David had already left and was milling around the corral, looking after the horses. Emily softly knocked, then opened the door and walked inside. She asked Sarah, "How are you feeling this morning?"

Sarah said, "I'm hurting a little. How much longer do you think before this baby comes?"

Emily said, "Let's have another look."

She examined Sarah again and found her to be dilated about six centimeters. It won't be long now. Do you think you could walk a little bit? It might help move things along."

Sarah answered, "I could try."

Emily found Sarah's dressing gown and helped her put it on. Then, she found some shoes and helped her put them on. They opened the door and began their stroll around the yard.

The men were down at the corral, seeing after the horses. Jake saw the women and bounded toward them with his tongue hanging out of his mouth and tail wagging furiously behind him. Emily and Sarah walked arm in arm as they made their way around the perimeter of the Sheboss Stand clearing. Sarah asked Emily about their new home in the valley. Emily told her of all they had built together in starting their homestead. She also told Sarah about how the Black Hand had attacked the Gordon farm after Daniel and Emily had left Sheboss Stand last time. Emily explained that Chief William Colbert and his braves had come to the rescue as Daniel and Emily joined in the fight against the Indians. Then she told how Chief William escorted them to their new home in the Water Valley.

As they continued their walk around the clearing, Sarah had to stop for a spell to overcome a contraction. The contractions were coming sooner and lingering for more extended periods. After thirty minutes or so, Sarah said, "I think I'd like to go back now."

Emily said, "Alright. Let's get you back."

As they began to walk back to the cabin, Sarah suddenly balked and said, "Oh! I think I just wet myself!"

Emily stopped and lifted Sarah's clothing up above her knees to check. Emily smiled at Sarah and said, "No, Dear. Your water just broke."

They continued back to the cabin, and Emily got Sarah settled back into her bed. She then washed her legs and pelvic area to make her a little more comfortable. Then Emily rechecked Sarah's belly. The contractions were nearly constant now.

"Emily! I think this baby is coming out now!"

"Hold on, Sarah! Don't push yet! This baby hasn't turned yet. I've got to try to move it around some. We don't want it to come into this world butt first."

Emily massaged Sarah's belly, pushing things around to get the baby to turn. Things weren't working out, however. She rechecked Sarah's pelvis. The baby was moving down the birth canal and was coming out bottom first. Emily knew that a breech baby could be a real problem. It could mean either Sarah's pelvis would not be large enough for the baby's head or that the baby could be in distress. The umbilical cord could be damaged or blocked, reducing oxygen flow to the baby. She had to act fast.

Emily ran out of the cabin and whistled, then called out, "Daniel! Come quick!"

Daniel and David ran from the corral to the cabin. Both men entered the house to see what was the matter. As they gathered around the bed, Emily instructed them. "Okay, Sarah. We've got a bit of a problem, but don't worry, I can fix this. I just need some help. Your baby is breech. You won't be able to deliver it normally, so I'm going to perform a C-section."

Sarah, with panic on her face, asked, "What's that?"

"I'm going to have to make an incision in your belly and remove the baby. I know it sounds scary, but we do it all the time in my old world."

Then Emily began barking orders. "David, I need you to heat some water on the stove. Daniel, once the water is heated, I need you to wash your hands with soap and water. We need more light. Can someone light another lamp?"

Both men did as Emily instructed. When the water had been heated, she and Daniel washed their hands in preparation for the procedure. Then Emily asked David for a piece of leather that Sarah could bite down on during the C-section. She prepared her instruments and asked Daniel to assist by handing her the correct instrument at the proper time.

Emily swabbed Sarah's belly with a betadine solution she had brought from 2018. Then she made an incision at the base of her stomach, slicing through tissue one layer at a time. Emily had to be careful not to injure the baby. Sarah winced in pain and screamed through a muffled voice. Once Emily had opened the womb, she was able to lift the baby out. She lay the baby on a towel, then tied off the umbilical cord with sutures.

"Daniel, take that bulb syringe and suck out the mucous from the baby's nose and mouth. Then clean him up with that towel."

Daniel did as instructed. While cleaning the baby, the baby seemed to come to life and began to cry. Daniel then realized that Emily had said, "*him*". He looked at David and said, "You have a son!"

Emily quickly stitched up the incisions she had made. Sarah had passed out from the pain and anxiety of the whole ordeal. Once Emily had finished, she washed away all the blood and placenta from Sarah. Emily then turned her attention to the baby. She checked him over thoroughly, counting his fingers and toes. Emily made sure he had not accidentally been nicked with her scalpel. She listened to his lungs and heart. Everything seemed to be just as it should. She placed the baby in a clean towel, wrapped him up, and then handed him to his father. "David, meet your son. Have you thought of a name for him?"

David smiled as he looked at his son, whom he held in his hands. "I will name him after Nafkl."

Daniel was puzzled at this. He had never heard David talk about having a brother.

"His name is Daniel."

Daniel was taken aback. He felt so honored that David would name his son after him. Emily beamed with the news. She looked at Daniel with tears of joy in her eyes. Then Emily turned her attention back to Sarah. She wet a towel with cold water, then wiped Sarah's brow. Eventually, Sarah awakened. Emily said, "Welcome back! Would you like to see your son?"

Sarah softly said, "Yes."

David brought the baby over to his wife and handed him over to her. The baby cried as his mother held him for the first time. Emily commented, "I'll bet he's hungry. You want to try to feed him?"

Sarah brought the baby to her breast and began to feed him. Emily turned to look at Daniel, then tossed her head toward the door, indicating it was time for him to leave. Daniel understood and walked outside. He sat down at the table in the dogtrot and wondered if he and Emily would ever have children. They had discussed it very little in the past. They both were so busy with their lives and careers that they had decided to wait. But things were different now. After seeing his namesake born and seeing David's reaction, Daniel decided it was the perfect time for them to become parents. He decided he would discuss it with Emily.

Two days later, Emily decided that it was time for them to head back home. Sarah and the baby were doing well. There was no sign of infection around the incision in Sarah's belly, the baby was eating well, and David was being an excellent nurse to Sarah and the baby. He held the baby as often as Sarah would allow him.

Emily and Daniel packed their gear, mounted their horses, and then turned them toward the trail leading to the Duck. They took their time as they rode. The morning was cold, but somehow, it didn't bother them as they rode together hand in hand. The warmth of each other's hands seemed to warm their whole bodies. Then, seemingly out of nowhere, Daniel asked Emily, "Are you ready?"

"Ready for what?" she asked.

"Ready to start making babies of our own."

"What, right here? Now?"

Daniel looked around then said, "Well, there's a nice quiet place over by those Dogwoods."

Emily scoffed and replied, "I can wait."

Then Daniel offered, "Seriously. I think it's about time we thought of having children of our own. What do you think?"

Emily thought for a while. She was silent for a moment, which made Daniel nervous. Then she said, "Sure. I'm ready. We can start."

Daniel reached over to Emily and gave her a kiss, which lingered for a while.

It was mid-afternoon when they unloaded from the ferry and made their way into the Gordon's encampment. Dolly exited the house as they rode up. She met them and asked Emily, "Would you mind checking on John? He's not feeling well."

Captain John Gordon had recently returned from his duties as General Andrew Jackson's army commander. He had served under Jackson for many years as they fought the Creeks in Mississippi and the British at the Battle of New Orleans. He returned in time to see the completion of their new Federal-style home that Dolly had been overseeing for over a year.

Emily replied, "Sure. I'd be happy to look in on him."

They dismounted, and while Daniel cared for the horses, Emily went into the house with Dolly. It was the first time Emily had met the captain. He was seated in the parlor, resting next to the fireplace. Dolly announced to the captain, "This is Emily Lane. She's a doctor, and I've asked her to examine you."

Emily started to correct Dolly but then decided it was no use. She was doing the work of a doctor. She would just let it go. "Do you mind, sir?" Emily asked.

"Do I have any choice?" he replied.

"No, you don't!" retorted Dolly.

The captain submitted to the examination. Emily listened to his heart and lungs and then checked his pulse. She felt the glands in his neck. She looked at his eyes, ears, nose, and mouth. Then she asked, "Do you smoke?"

"Every chance I get!"

"Do you drink?"

"Not as often as I'd like!"

"Have you been feeling any tightness in your chest or difficulty breathing?"

"No more than usual!"

Dolly added, "He's just been so tired ever since he got back.

Emily said, "Well, Captain Gordon, your heart isn't beating as it should. Your lungs don't sound too clear either. My guess is you've lived a hard life for a long time, and your body is trying to tell you to slow down. I know it won't do me any good to tell you to lay off the smoking and drinking. Just try to keep it to a minimum. Get as much rest as you can. No more traveling for a while. Stay here and enjoy this nice house that you and Dolly have built."

Dolly walked Emily to the door and asked, "How much do I owe you, Emily?"

"Not a thing. After all you have done for Daniel and me, I could never think of charging you for my services."

Dolly replied, "Well, thanks. Tell you what though, when you and Daniel get ready to build your cabin, I'll send some of my boys over to help you out."

"That would be wonderful. I think Daniel plans to start in early May. He and Tommy are cutting and preparing logs right now."

Dolly said, "Well, I'll send them over then. Are you going to stay the night or keep riding?"

"I think we're going to keep going," Emily replied. "It looks like it will be a clear night. We shouldn't have too much trouble."

"Well, thanks again," Dolly said. "If you should need anything, give us a holler."

Chapter 4

May 5, 1819

As the sun peeked over the horizon on the east end of the Water Valley, the sky glowed a magnificent array of colors ranging from deep orange to gold, fading into clear azure skies. Daniel watched in awe as he cradled his second cup of coffee in his hands, watching as nature painted its picture, displaying the beauty of God's creation. Emily walked up from behind him and wrapped her arms around his waist. "Are you glad we stayed?" she asked.

"I can't imagine ever going back," he replied.

Daniel, Emily, and Tommy Brown had been working all winter, cutting Cedars that grew along the valley's edge. The two mules, Rusty and Pepper, easily pulled the logs out of the forest and into the valley. The trees that Daniel and Tommy had cut ranged from 8 to 12 inches in diameter. They stacked the logs close to their building site, allowing them to cure. The creek bed and the bank of the Duck River would provide mud that they would mix with broom straw sage, which grew wild in the valley, to make chinking for the house's log walls. Today would be their first day of actual construction.

When spring arrived, Daniel and Tommy took a break from logging to plant seventy-five acres of corn. They also broke enough ground near the cabin site for Emily to plant a vegetable garden. Daniel had used part of the money that Emily brought with her to purchase enough seed to plant the cornfield. Emily planted a vegetable garden with heirloom seeds she had brought through the Shimmering. She knew that seeds from the twenty-first century were engineered or hybrid seeds. They produced excellent crops of beautiful vegetables, but the seeds from those vegetables were useless to save for replanting. It was sort of like trying to get Rusty and Pepper to reproduce.

Tommy Brown exited his tent to join Daniel and Emily by the fire. Emily fixed him a cup of coffee and greeted him, "Good morning, Tommy!"

He replied, "Mornin', Em'ly!"

Tommy made the trip with Emily through the Shimmering. He had been a park ranger and helped Emily search for Daniel when Daniel and his friend Jimbo went missing. Tommy was tall and thin - about five feet, eleven inches tall, weighing around 170 pounds. But he had gained a lot of muscle during the past few months, working with Daniel, harvesting the Cedars, and plowing the fields. Tommy was soft-spoken and a man of few words but had proven to be very loyal, especially toward Emily.

Emily fried up some bacon and eggs for their breakfast. She had been saving up her eggs, knowing she would need every one of the three dozen eggs to feed the crew that had come to help raise their new log house. The smell of bacon awoke the campers from their sleep. One by one, more heads began poking out of the tents that they had erected the night before. Dolly Gordon had sent seven children to help the Lanes raise their cabin. Micah, the youngest boy, was the first to make his way over to the fire in search of the delicious-smelling bacon and eggs. The rest of the clan soon followed him. James, who was eighteen, the twins, Mark and Luke were nineteen, Evan was twenty, and John Jr was twenty-two. They also brought Amy, who was now fourteen, along. Amy begged to come because she was smitten with Tommy Brown.

After breakfast, the construction of Daniel and Emily's new home began. The mules dragged large limestone rocks from the riverbed to create a foundation for the house. Emily and Amy were in charge of the mules. Pepper and Rusty were quite familiar with a woman's gentle yet firm hand, so they were very accepting of Amy when she took the lead of their halter at any given time. All eight of the men worked together, preparing the logs for stacking. Four men squared up the logs using adz, hatchets, and axes. Two other men started notching the logs' ends to be stacked together like Lincoln Logs to give the house its shape. The cabin faced northwest because Emily wanted to be able to walk out of the front door and view the Duck River and Beaver Creek at the same time. Tommy and Daniel worked together with the women to stack the logs. Poles were placed strategically at the end of each run of logs to be used as skids. They pulled logs up the skids to put them on top of the walls. They looped a rope around the end of each log, then hitched it to one of the mules. The mules would walk forward, sliding the log up the skids until they reached their destination on the wall. By the end of the first day, they had completed four runs.

The next morning, Daniel was awakened by Jake, who rumbled a low growl deep in his throat. Daniel knew that meant either someone or something was encroaching on their grounds. Daniel picked up his rifle and exited the tent, trying not to wake Emily. She was breathing deeply, indicating that she was fast asleep. Daniel whispered to the dog, "What is it, Jake?"

Daniel fixed his eyes to the position where Jake was staring. To the east of their camp, seventy-five yards away, was a group of six deer. Four does, and two bucks were grazing along the bank of the Beaver. Daniel slowly and carefully walked to the side of the cabin and stood at one of the eastern corner runs. He raised his rifle, rested it on the top run, and bent down to sight his gun at one of the deer. Jake grew impatient, and his growl grew louder. "Hush, Jake!" Daniel scolded in a loud whisper. Daniel lined up his sights on the rifle at one of the bucks, took a deep breath, slowly let it out, and squeezed the trigger. **BOOM**! The lead projectile exploded from the rifle's barrel and met its mark. The buck dropped immediately, dying where he had stood. The other deer scattered for a moment, and then all ran toward the same opening in the forest making their escape.

Daniel's shot caused everyone in the camp to jump, startled from their bedrolls. The men grabbed their rifles and leaped from their tents, ready for battle with whomever or whatever might be attacking the camp. Knowing that he had awoken the whole group, Daniel quickly raised his arms over his head while holding his rifle and yelled to them, "Ho! It's just me!"

Everyone began talking and asking questions at the same time, so Daniel couldn't understand anything they said. He knew, however, what was on their minds. He pointed to the east and said, "I shot a deer."

They all looked toward the position where Daniel was pointing and saw Jake sprinting toward a carcass lying motionless next to the Beaver Branch.

Daniel went into his tent and retrieved his hunting knife. As he headed out to fetch his prey, Evan said, "I'll go with you."

Daniel nodded in agreement, and the two of them jogged toward the deer, Evan carrying his rifle, which was still loaded. They found Jake sniffing the remains of the buck as they arrived. He licked at the open wound a little to taste the fresh blood leaking from the bullet hole. Daniel took out his knife and jabbed it into the base of the deer's neck and sliced through one of the main arteries, causing the blood to flow freely from the deer's body. As they waited for the body to empty itself of the thick, red liquid, Evan said, "That was a good shot. Where did you learn to shoot like that?"

Daniel replied, "David Colbert."

"The Indian up at Sheboss?"

"Yeah, that's him. I once saw him shoot the head off of a turkey from seventy-five feet away," Daniel bragged. "David taught me everything I know about survival."

Daniel then looked at Evan and asked, "Can you help me lift it to my shoulders?"

Evan laid his rifle on the ground and lifted the front end of the deer from the ground. Daniel knelt and dipped his head and shoulders underneath the deer to position it across his shoulders. He then carefully stood and hopped a little, causing the deer to jump to a new position on his shoulders so it would be more balanced. As the two of them returned to camp, along with Jake, Evan remembered something. "Daniel, I just remembered. Maw had me bring something to you that belonged to Gus. He left it behind with her when he went through the Shimmering. I guess she thought you should have it since you and Gus were so close."

Daniel asked, "Well, what is it?"

"It's just an old shoulder bag he left behind. I don't know what's in it. I didn't look."

When they got back to the camp, they found everyone stirring around, getting ready to begin their long day of work. The deer was a welcome sight. It would provide meat for them for at least a couple of days. Daniel and Micah began dressing out the deer. As they removed all of the internal organs, they handed the heart, kidney, and liver over to Amy, who cleaned them, sliced them up, and fried them for breakfast. After they dressed the deer, they skinned it. James removed the head from the hide and proceeded to extract the brain. They intended to use the brains for tanning the leather. Daniel, Micah, Luke, and Mark all began stripping the hide of any remaining fat. They all made quick work of it. They then rolled the pelt, placed it in a large clay jar, and filled it with water. James made a paste from the brains and put it in a glass jar to store. Once the deerskin had soaked in water for a few days, they would use the paste for tanning the hide.

After breakfast, Micah returned to his tent, retrieved the shoulder bag, and handed it to Daniel. Daniel examined the bag. It was ancient but well-maintained. Someone had made it from animal skin, possibly beaver. The leather was soft and pliable. The outside of the bag was dark brown. Daniel opened the flap of the bag and looked inside. He reached into the haversack and pulled out the contents one by one. Daniel found a small knife, about four inches in length. The handle was carved from animal bone. He then pulled out a small glass bottle. He uncorked the top and found that the bottle's contents were some sort of black liquid. "It's ink!" said Micah.

Daniel nodded his head with understanding and reinserted the cork into the container. He then pulled a large feather from the bag—a quill pen made from a turkey feather. The last thing he pulled from the sack was a book. It was almost as large as the bag—Daniel guessed it to be about seven inches by ten inches. It was leather-bound, but the leather was old, worn, and water-stained.

Daniel carefully opened the book. Inside, on the first page, he read,

The Diary of Gus Childers

Tears came to Daniel's eyes as he realized he held the contents of many unanswered questions in his hand. Gus and Daniel had become very close during their last three months together. But most of the time was spent with Gus asking questions about Daniel's life. Daniel had learned very little about Gus's life. Daniel carefully closed the book and placed it back in the bag. He would read it later while no one else was around.

CHAPTER 5

While Micah and James finished dressing out the deer, Amy prepared a pot of deer stew and put it on the fire for their lunch. Everyone else resumed working on the cabin. Emily and John Jr. handled the mules while the rest of the Gordon boys continued preparing logs to be stacked. Tommy and Daniel stacked the logs. By noon, they had managed to raise four more runs onto the cabin walls. The last run was complete by nightfall, and the gable ends were halfway done.

That night, after supper, Emily noticed Amy and Tommy having a conversation at the edge of the camp. Amy was doing most of the talking. Tommy seemed a little uncomfortable, continually looking back toward the others to see who might be watching. When everyone else had made their way into their tents and Amy had finally said *"goodnight"* to Tommy, Emily motioned for Tommy to come and sit with her.

"How's it going, Tommy?" she asked.

"Aw it's goin' fine, I guess," he replied.

Emily lowered her voice as she began speaking. "That Amy is quite the talker, isn't she?"

Tommy looked back over his shoulder to make sure no one was listening. "Yes, ma'am, she is."

Emily asked, "Do you like her?"

Even in the dark of night, Emily could see that Tommy was blushing.

"Aw well, she's right purdy for such a young thang."

Then Emily said, "Tommy, you need to ask that girl to marry you."

Tommy was shocked at such a suggestion and caught himself before he blurted out, then only whispered, "Marry her! I couldn't do that. She's only fourteen years old. I'm more than ten years older than her. Why they'd arrest me for even thinkin' such a thing."

"Tommy," Emily responded. "We're not living in the 21st century anymore. Things are different now than they were - will be -," she corrected herself, "in 2019. Girls in these times get married as early as thirteen. I can clearly see that Amy Gordon has set her sights on you."

Tommy thought for a moment, then asked, "Well, where would we live? I don't have nothin' to offer her as a husband. No place to live, no job, nothin'."

Emily smiled and said, "Tommy, you can set up right here with me and Daniel. This place is going to be way too big for just the two of us. We've got more than 200 acres of bottomland that will need planting and tending to. Daniel needs a partner, and I could teach Amy about medicine so she can assist me when I need it."

Emily pointed to the east and said, "We'll build the two of you a cabin right over there near the Beaver. Not too close, but not too far, either. So, what do you think?"

Tommy's mood lightened a bit as he asked, "What should I do? Should I just ask her?"

Emily said, "Well, you need to talk to her folks, first. When we're finished building this cabin and when the Gordon's go back home, you can ride back with them. Talk to Dolly and see if Captain John is feeling well enough for you to speak with him. If he is, ask him. If she says he's not doing well enough, ask Dolly for permission to marry Amy. If they ask how you plan to make your living, just tell them you've been made a full partner in our homestead."

Daniel lit a candle in his tent and took the opportunity to look at Gus's diary while Emily and Tommy were talking outside. Daniel examined the book more carefully. It was leather-bound, and although it was ancient, it had been well preserved. Gus must have kept it rubbed down with linseed oil or saddle soap because the leather was still soft. The pages were not in as good condition. The edges of some of the pages were well-worn, ragged, and water-stained. Daniel opened the book to the first page.

The Diary of Gus Childers

Daniel noticed that the name Gus Childers had been written in at a later point. The original had since been marked through. Daniel wondered about the name. Gus had told him that his name was August Moon Earthchild. He was born to parents who were hippies. They had moved from the San Francisco, California, area to Summertown, Tennessee, when he was a boy. He and his friend Robbie came through the Shimmering in 1973, but Robbie was killed almost immediately by Ilbok Losa. Ilbok Losa was the Chickasaw name for the Black Hand, the renegade group of Chickasaws who were followers of Chief George Colbert. George Colbert was the half-brother to William Colbert, the chief who Emily had nursed back to health after he had contracted influenza. Although William and his younger brother George had fought with the British against the colonists in the late 1700s, they didn't see eye to eye on many things.

While William was more contemporary in his thinking, George was more of a traditionalist. William was flamboyant and known to indulge in "liquid spirits," while George was against drinking whiskey. He wanted his people to observe the old ways. Ilbok Losa were members of George's tribe.

Daniel turned the page in the diary and found its first entry.

My name is August Moon Earthchild. I found this book by a river bed inside a leather bag. I don't know who it belonged to. I will use it to give an account of my time in this new world I have entered. I have tried to keep a count of the days that I have been here. I calculate it to be 22 days. If my count is correct, then today should be July 13th. I don't know how I got here. All I know is I must have gone through a time portal of some sort. I don't know what year it is.

The only people I have seen are the ones who killed my friend Robbie. They were dressed as Indians. I found another group riding down the river in canoes the next day. I pray that they do not see me. I have spent most of my time along the river. I think it is the Duck unless I have been transported to a completely different world. I've been

surviving so far on berries and nuts. I retrieved the spear that was used to kill Robbie, but I have been unable to kill any wild game yet. If I don't figure out how to catch game soon, I will starve this winter. I hope to find civilization at some point, but for now, I will just try to stay alive.

A. E.

P.S. I wish I could awaken from this nightmare. I want to go home!

Tears formed at the corners of Daniel's eyes as he read the first entry. How frightened Gus must have been. He was only sixteen years old when he came through the Shimmering. He had just witnessed the brutal murder of his best friend and was now stranded in a time and place of which he was unfamiliar.

CHAPTER 6

June 22, 1773

August woke from a restless sleep. His skin was sore and bloody from the blackberry thorns that had pierced his body while he lay in hiding from the painted men. When August first roused, he thought maybe it had all been a dream. He raised his head and carefully looked toward the clearing where Robbie's body lay. No luck. His body was still there. The painted man's lance was still sticking out of the chest of his beloved friend. August remembered trying to move the body last night under cover of darkness, but he didn't have the strength.

Cautiously, August moved back into the open field. He scanned the area, looking for any movement. Crows were cawing in the treetops. Mockingbirds were singing, and bluejays were cawing. He decided that the birds would stop their singing if anyone were out there waiting for him. He hoped so, anyway. He walked over to Robbie, grasped the lance, and tried to remove it from his body. Whenever he pulled on the spear, Robbie's body lifted off the ground with it. So, August placed his left sneaker-covered foot against Robbie, then tugged on the lance. The spear slowly his friend's exited the lifeless body until it was, at last, free.

August started to throw the spear away, deep into the forest, so that no one would find it. But then, he decided it might come in handy. The painted men might return. He could use it for protection.

He tried once more to drag Robbie from the clearing. He managed, through much effort, to haul him into a thicketed area of honeysuckle.

The vines quickly entangled August as he tried to move through them. He finally gave up and left Robbie in the thicket. He decided to look for some large rocks to cover Robbie's body like a grave. He didn't have a shovel to dig a proper grave, and the spear would be of little use as a digging tool in the ground so riddled with limestone. He spent the next few hours searching for and collecting stones. He found that by locating groves of cedar trees, he could find lots of large rocks that would be suitable. The roots of the cedars had worked their way through large segments of limestone, causing them to break apart over time and creating smaller, more manageable stones for him to carry. With the sun at its highest point in the sky, August finally had covered his friend with enough limestone to keep scavengers from desecrating his body. Before burying him, August searched Robbie's pockets for the keys to the VW bus that they had driven from Summertown. When he found them, he put them in his pocket, then covered Robbie with the stones.

August sat down to rest and munched on some of the blackberries he had picked the day before. *"I need to get back home to get someone to help me get Robbie back to the Grove,"* he thought. The Grove was the commune where his family and many other families had settled just a few years earlier.

He picked up the spear and the five-gallon bucket containing the blackberries, then proceeded south. It was just past noon, so the sun was only starting to dip toward the west. He turned so the sun rested just above his right shoulder, and he walked through the forest. It was nothing like he had remembered from yesterday. There should have been an open area within twenty feet of his location, but it was nowhere to be found. He continued as best he could, moving through the thick growth of trees, ferns, and vines. He checked the sun's location once in a while to ensure he stayed on course. After an hour or so, he could hear the water moving in the distance. He thought it must be the Duck River if he was still going in the right direction. Once he found the Duck, he could eventually move farther west to find the Natchez Trace Parkway. The mid-summer heat was beating down on him, and he hadn't drunk anything all day. He decided to find the bank of the river to see if it might have water clean enough for him to drink.

When he reached the water's edge, he found himself standing on a bluff about twelve feet above the river. His eyes moved right and left, searching for a more natural path to the river. Fifteen yards to the west, he found what he was looking for. A fallen hickory tree, uprooted most likely from heavy winds, was dipping down toward the river bank from the top of the bluff. August slinked through briars and honeysuckle vines to reach the makeshift stairway down. Once he reached the tree, he tested it for strength. It had evidently been in this position for some time because there were very few leaves on the branches of the giant tree. What few leaves were still attached had all died long ago.

Once satisfied with the tree's strength, he prepared to shimmy down the tree trunk feet first. He first set the bucket of blackberries down at the base of the tree along with the spear he had removed from Robbie's body. As he wrapped his arms around the tree trunk to navigate to the ground, the bark cut into the bare skin on his arms - not enough to make them bleed, but sufficient to blister his arms, much like a carpet burn. When he had worked his way down close enough to the ground that he was only about six feet from the bottom, he let go with his legs and hung there momentarily before releasing his grip on the tree. "Ooff!" he cried out, but not too loudly. The drop had been a little farther than he had anticipated. He landed on all fours, slowly raising himself as he found his balance.

Cautiously, August moved to the bank of the river, watching for movement in all directions. He bent down close to the water, then waited and listened. The river was quite noisy as it rushed past him, flowing east to west. The water was clear. It was much cleaner than he had remembered the Duck River as having been. *"Maybe this isn't the Duck after all,"* he thought to himself. He cupped his hands together and dipped them into the water. The water was cold and soothing to his skin. He brought his hands up to his face and sipped the cooling liquid. He did this several times until he had quenched his thirst. He then dipped his hands into the water and splashed it onto his face, washing away the sweat. He washed his head, then worked his way down, cleaning his arms. He cringed as the water ran over his blistered arms. They hurt, but the cold water began to relieve the pain.

August raised himself up when he realized he hadn't checked his surroundings lately. He sat quietly and searched the far bank. His heart jumped when he heard a voice far off in the distance. He decided the voice was coming from the east. But not just one voice. As the sound came closer, he could hear more than one. He quickly searched for a place to hide. He looked up at the fallen Hickory tree and decided it would take too long to climb it. There was very little brush at this section of the bank. Then he saw it. He decided to go into the water and hide beneath the branches that dipped down into the water's edge. He then realized that his tie-dyed shirt would be seen too easily. He quickly pulled the shirt off over his head, then searched for a place to hide it. He looked up again and tried to throw it back onto the bluff. He rolled it up into a tight ball and threw it as high and far as possible. The shirt disappeared at the top. August spun around and quickly but quietly slid into the water underneath the tree branches. He held onto one of the tree branches, trying not to be swept away by the water's current. His heart was pounding, and he soon began shivering because of the cold waters and his fear.

It wasn't long before he saw them. There were five dugout canoes, each holding two men, riding the current down the river. They continued conversing with each other in a tongue August didn't recognize. They were all naked from the waist up and had long dark hair. August noted, however, that they weren't painted like the men who had killed Robbie. It didn't matter to him, though. He wasn't about to expose himself to anyone at this point. As far as he was concerned, everyone was an enemy.

August waited under cover of the branches. Five minutes seemed like an hour to him as he waited for the sounds of their voices to fade entirely away. He slowly began to climb from underneath the branches of the fallen Hickory tree. His long, flowing hair became entangled in the limbs, making climbing out of the water quite challenging. When he finally stood on dry land, his bell-bottom jeans weighed him down, making climbing the tree difficult. He removed his jeans and wrung them out as best he could. Daylight was fading, so August decided to find a place to hold up for the night. He stretched his jeans out on top of the fallen tree, hoping they would not be conspicuous to a passerby. August then climbed back up the tree while wearing only his boxers. He gathered the things he had left on top of the bluff; then August returned to the river's bank. Once his body had dried, he pulled the shirt back on to help keep him comfortable during the night. August had no matches and no flint with which to make fire. He wasn't sure he would even know how if he had. He munched on blackberries and drank from the river until he had his fill. August felt his eyelids grow heavy as the sun dipped underneath the horizon and the moon began to rise. He curled beneath the fallen Hickory and fell into a deep sleep.

Chapter 7

May 8, 1819

The day began as the sun rose at the east end of the Water Valley. Daniel and his crew stirred from their tents. Emily was already slicing and cooking bacon over the fire, and biscuits were resting in the Dutch oven. Daniel strolled over to Emily and wrapped his arms around her from behind. "Why didn't you wake me?" he asked.

"You looked like you needed the extra sleep," she said. "You were tossing a lot last night."

"Yeah, I was dreaming about Gus. Can you imagine being sixteen years old and tossed into an unknown world with nothing to help you survive except your wits? He was in the middle of the wilderness, his best friend had been killed right before his eyes, and he had nowhere to go for safety. This country was literally unseen by white men at that time. It would be two years before Daniel Boone and his men began cutting the trail through Tennessee and Kentucky, and all of that would be north of here."

As the rest of the crew began meandering toward the fire, Daniel changed the subject. "Good morning, Tommy. Did you sleep well?"

Tommy responded, "I guess."

Daniel said as everyone else wandered up to the fire, "Good morning, everyone."

All the others mumbled their "*Good mornings*" to him.

As they all gathered their biscuits and bacon, along with a hot cup of coffee, Daniel began making assignments for the day. "John, would you and Evan start cutting the shakes for the roof? The rest of you can divide up into two teams and start collecting rocks for the fireplace while Tommy and I start nailing up the shakes."

Once they all finished their breakfast, they began their assigned task.

Tommy and Daniel climbed the roof and nailed the decking boards onto the rafters. Four rafters were attached the previous day to the long, sturdy ridge pole that ran from one end of the cabin to the other. Then, the decking boards were placed on top of the rafters. The deck boards were made from smaller trees that the men split down the middle. They ran down the length of the house and were attached with the rounded side up. They would give a beautiful flat covering inside the house as a ceiling and give the men a surface outside to nail up the shakes.

John and Evan used some of the smaller logs to make the cedar shakes. They sawed them into lengths of about sixteen inches, then split the small logs using an L-shaped tool with a blade on one side called a froe. The edge was hammered into the end of a short log, causing it to split along the wood grain. It produced an ideal covering for the top of the cabin.

The rest of the gang split up into two teams. Emily worked with Luke and Micah, while Amy worked with James and Mark. Each group had a mule and a sled made from split logs. They began searching up and down the Duck River and Beaver Branch to find large pieces of limestone suitable for building a fireplace and chimney. Although the sleds were quite heavy, Pepper and Rusty easily pulled them even while laden with large limestone boulders. The men carried iron pry bars that were five feet long to use as levers to remove the limestone buried in the soil after centuries of rain and erosion. Limestone was plentiful here, so it didn't take long for the crew to gather enough to build the chimney and then some. When the time came, they would probably have enough to make Tommy's chimney.

Once the rocks had been collected, Mark and Luke began shaping the stones into blocks by chipping them with hammers and chisels. Hitting the limestone in just the right spot would cause the unwanted pieces of limestone to break away, leaving nearly flat surfaces. John and Evan began stacking the rocks along the west end of the cabin to form a chimney. Because the stones were shaped into blocks, they could dry-stack them into the desired design. They would come back afterward and fill the spaces between the bricks with mortar to seal the edges.

After finishing the roof, Daniel and Tommy began cutting out sections of the log walls to add windows, a door, and an opening for the chimney. The windows would be open with shutters on the outside that could be closed during colder weather.

The rest of the crew collected more mud and straw to make chinking. The chinking sealed the spaces in between the logs that had been stacked for the walls. By the end of the fifth day, the cabin was completed. The crew even built a table and benches to fit inside the cabin for dining. Daniel and John Jr. built a rope bed so Emily and Daniel wouldn't have to sleep on the floor. Emily and Amy made the mattress by sewing together quilts. Eventually, Emily could make a proper mattress by using goose down.

Around six that evening, the men wandered down to the bank of the Duck. There, they went swimming to wash the week's worth of sweat and grime from their bodies. The women stayed behind and chose to bathe further east in the shallow waters of Beaver Branch, out of sight from the men.

James and Micah demonstrated to Daniel the art of catching catfish by sticking their arms into underwater holes in the river bank and waiting for the fish to bite them. Daniel had seen this before, but not in person. He had seen "noodling" performed on television but had never attempted it himself. He wasn't particularly ready to try it now, either. It just didn't appeal to him. It wasn't long before James and Micah had captured enough of the whiskered creatures to feed the whole crew for supper that night.

Evan grabbed one of the fish and pulled out his knife to begin cleaning the creature. Daniel asked, "How do you plan on preparing that fish for cooking?"

Evan replied, "The only way I know how. I skin it first, then gut it and remove the head."

Daniel then asked, "Do you mind if I show you how to fillet the critter without having to gut it? Its cleaner and easier than trying to skin it too."

Evan looked at Daniel, somewhat amazed, and replied, "By all means."

Daniel took out his knife and laid the fish on a stump nearby. He sliced through the fish's side just behind its head, all the way to its backbone. Daniel then carefully slid his knife along the vertebrae all the way down to the tail. He flicked his wrist, causing the blade to flip the piece of meat over the back of the tail, revealing the meaty side of the fillet. Daniel then slid the knife between the flesh and the skin until the meat was completely free. He flipped the fish over and did the same with its other side. In a matter of thirty seconds, he had two perfectly prepared fillets. All of the Gordons gawked and remarked how simple the procedure was. Everyone pulled out their *own* knives and gave it a try. Happily, they walked back to camp to show the women what they had learned.

Emily was excited to see the catfish fillets. She breaded the fillets with a mixture of flour, cornmeal, salt, and pepper and fried them in a skillet with hot, bubbling lard. She boiled potatoes in a pot to serve with them and also made cornbread pancakes. Amy prepared beans using canned pintos, canned tomatoes, bacon, and brown sugar. They all had quite a feast as they happily ate their last meal together before the Gordons went home the next day.

After supper, Tommy and Amy took a private walk along the bank of Beaver Branch. Everyone else huddled around the fire, admiring the cabin they had all worked so hard to build while making small talk. At some point in the conversation, Micah nodded toward the couple as they strode away and said, "Looks like Amy found herself a beau."

The other brothers all smiled and chuckled a little. John responded, "He seems like a nice feller. He's a good hard worker, too."

He then looked at Emily and asked, "Do you think they'll get married?"

Emily replied, "I think so. I know Tommy would like to marry her, but he is a little uncomfortable being around a young lady who is so much younger than he."

Emily changed the subject by asking John, "How is your father doing?"

John said, "He's pretty weak. Ma says he's just worn out."

Emily responded, "Well, war can do that to a man. Maybe I should go back with you tomorrow and check on him."

John said, "I'm sure he and Ma both would appreciate that."

Daniel approached Emily and asked, "Would you like to see our new home, Mrs. Lane?"

Emily smiled at him and responded, "Well, of course I would, Mr. Lane."

The two of them walked hand in hand back to the cabin and stepped up on the porch. Daniel opened the door, then stepped aside to allow Emily to enter first. The sun was lowering over the tops of the trees, and daylight was fading. However, there was still enough light shining through the opened window and opened the doorway for Emily to see inside. The furnishings were sparse. Just the table and chairs and the rope bed that sat in the corner of the room. Daniel had retrieved the blankets from their bedrolls from the tent while Emily was preparing the evening meal and brought them into the cabin to set up their sleeping quarters. Emily's eyes lit up in dimmed light as she saw the bed. "It's perfect!" Then she reached up and kissed him.

When she pulled away from Daniel to look at him, she noticed a look of concern on his face. "What's wrong?" she asked.

Daniel replied, "I overheard you asking John about his father. Do you plan to go back with them tomorrow?"

Emily answered, "Well, yes. I thought I might be able to help him. Why?

Daniel said, "Emily, I don't mind if you go and check on him. But, you won't be able to do much for him. He'll be dead in a little more than a month."

Emily exclaimed, "Oh, Daniel! Maybe I can do something to change that. How does he die?"

Daniel replied, "I don't know. History doesn't provide that information. And, besides, I'm not sure it's a good idea for you to try to change things like that. If you want to go and try to make him more comfortable, then I'll understand. But don't try to change history."

Emily lowered her head in contemplation and turned away from Daniel so he couldn't see the tears beginning to run down her cheeks. She sniffled and asked, "When will he die?"

Daniel replied, "June sixteenth, but don't tell Dolly. Don't tell anyone, please."

"Alright.", she responded. "I won't. But I'd still like to go back with the Gordon's tomorrow and see what I can do for him."

CHAPTER 8

The next morning, there seemed to be a bit of excitement in the air as everyone rose from their beds. Emily and Amy prepared breakfast while the Gordon men started packing up their camp.

After breakfast, the Gordons saddled and packed their horses to prepare for the trip home. Emily saddled her mare, and Tommy saddled up the Sorrel. He also packed the Black that Daniel had claimed from his assailants at Sheboss Stand last year. All of them mounted their horses except Emily. She walked over to Daniel while leading her horse.

She asked, "Are you sure you don't mind my going to the Gordon Place to check on the captain?"

Daniel answered, "Not at all. Just remember what I told you. Make him comfortable if you can. But, don't expect to keep him from the inevitable."

"I'll remember," Emily said. "You can expect us back in a few days, maybe longer if Tommy has trouble finding the words to ask for Amy's hand."

The two of them snickered, then embraced. "I love you.", she said.

"I love you, too.", he replied.

Emily mounted the mare and joined the others by the Beaver Creek as they crossed together and began the journey back to the Gordon House. They would take a little less than a day to make the trip.

Daniel found plenty to keep himself busy while Emily was gone. He and Jake went hunting on the first day. It was more of a hike than a hunt.

They explored the hillside that surrounded the valley. Daniel saw rabbits, squirrels, and even a doe, but he didn't feel much like killing anything. He just wanted to enjoy the quiet of being alone for a while.

Over the next two days, he spent time making sure everything was working fine around the farm. He checked on the corn to see how well it was growing. He also took a ride down the valley toward Leiper's Creek just to enjoy the ride.

After supper on the third night, Daniel picked up Gus's diary and walked out to the front porch. He took with him a candle and lit it as he sat down on the edge of the porch. He opened the book and began reading at the place where he had last finished.

October 2, 1773

I now know the date and the place that I now abide in. After spending much of my time by the river trying to survive, I have developed enough skill with the spear to at least catch fish from time to time. The fish and the blackberries and blueberries that I have been able to gather have kept me alive.

Thirty-two days ago, I decided to leave my little camp at the river, which I now know to be the Duck River, and headed north and east. I stayed as close to the creeks and rivers as possible, following them upstream. Two days ago, I came across a trapper who was setting traps along the bank of what he told me was the Cumberland River. His name is Jasques-Timothee' Boucher de Montbrun. He said I could call him Timothy.

He has a camp set up in a cave that sits on a bluff right above the river. He said I could work for him and he gave me some warmer clothes to wear. Tomorrow, he said, we will go to the salt lick to hunt for some wild game so he can harvest their hides.

He has been accommodating but also a man of ill temper when things don't go his way. I am just happy to have someone to talk to again. I miss my family.

September 1773

The summer heat beat down upon August as he made his trek through the brush that grew along the river he had been following for five days. He used the spearhead to hack his way through the briars and honeysuckle vines that grew in his path. His old Converse sneakers, which had once been bright white, now were a filthy brown. The shoes barely covered his feet. He had lost weight over the past few weeks, which caused his bell-bottom Levi's to hang loosely from his hips. He no longer wore his tie-dyed T-shirt. He carried it in the leather bag draped over his head and shoulder.

His supplies of berries and nuts had run out two days ago. He managed to find only a few blueberries to nibble on as he traveled down his makeshift trail. His feet were heavy, and August was fatigued and hungry. His mouth was as dry as sandpaper. He decided to take a break at the river's edge, just at a point where it bent to the east. He lay prostrate on the bank with his face in the water. The cold liquid revived him only a little. He sucked in the water through his parched lips, then rolled over to his back and allowed the stream to flow through his long mangled hair. He decided he could go no further. He would lie here and die, never to see his mother or father ever again. He closed his eyes and drifted off to sleep.

August felt apprehensive all of a sudden. He opened his eyes and discovered that he was being held down on the ground by men. They wouldn't let him move. They were speaking to him in a language he did not understand. He struggled to get up, but their grip on his arms was too firm, and he was weak from hunger. One of the men brought out a tomahawk and, raised it above his head and prepared to swing it down toward August's skull. August's eyes widened in fear and the realization that he was about to die. He struggled with all of his might and screamed out, "Don't kill me! Don't kill me!"

Then, he felt his body rock back and forth, from side to side. He faintly heard a voice speaking to him. The voice came from off in the distance but slowly came closer until, finally, he was able to listen to the words spoken to him.

"English? You are English? Are you all alright? Wake up, boy!"

August woke with a start. He opened his eyes to see a man in his mid-twenties looking down upon him. The man was dressed as a frontiersman. His hair was long, although not as long as August's, and was tied back with a leather thong. He wore a beard that was scruffy and black. His voice was rough sounding, and he spoke with an accent. *"French?"* Gus asked himself.

The man took hold of August's arm and lifted him to a sitting position. "Sit up, mon ami."

August asked him, "Are you, French?"

The man replied, "Oui! Yes, I am French. More precisely, French Canadian."

August asked, "Who are you? What are you doing here?"

The man replied, "Ah! I should ask you the same. But that is okay. I will go first. I am Jacques-Timothée Boucher, Sieur de Montbrun, but you may call me Timothy. I am from Canada, and I am a trapper. Now, how about you?"

August looked at the man and tried to say something about himself that wouldn't sound crazy. "My name is August Moon Earthchild. I've been lost in the forest for weeks. I came here from the southwest, hoping to find civilization."

"How did you become lost? Where are your people?" asked Timothy.

August replied, "I don't know. My friend and I came to this place where we were looking for berries. All of a sudden, he was killed by Indians. I don't know how we got here or how to get home. I don't even know where I am now."

Timothy replied, "Well, August Moon Earthchild, you are in the Cumberland valley. This river is the Cumberland River. The year is 1773, and you have a very long and strange name. Believe this from a man whose name is even longer and stranger than your own. You should think of shortening it just as I have done. How about . . . Gus? And Earthchild is much too strange. Let's see . . . Earth . . . Child . . . how about Childers? You should be called Gus Childers."

August thought for a moment about Timothy's suggestion. He didn't much like changing his name. It was the name his parents had given him. However, he also knew that a name like August Moon Earthchild would stand out and might create problems for him in 1773. After all, there weren't any hippies in 1773.

August replied, "Okay. Gus Childers, it is."

Timothy smiled and responded, "Yes? Oui?"

"Oui!" replied Gus.

Timothy said, "Tres bon! Now, let us get you to my cave, and we will find you some proper clothing."

Chapter 9

Daniel's eyes began to droop. He was tired from the day's events. He thought of Gus's entry in the diary. He recognized the name Jacques-Timothée Boucher, Sieur de Montbrun. He was better known in middle Tennessee as Timothy Demonbreun. Demonbreun has a street and a bridge named after him in Nashville, in the downtown district. He had inhabited the Cumberland Valley before any other white man. Demonbreun was a fur trapper for part of the year while living in a cave about a mile north of the area that would be settled as Fort Nashboro in 1779. He also served as Justice of the Peace for a small village in Illinois called Kaskaskia. Sometime during this period, it is believed that his wife was captured by Indians. No record existed of her for eight to ten years. After the American Revolutionary War, her name was listed once again on record in Illinois. Demonbreun served under George Rogers Clark during the revolution and was later appointed Lt. Governor of Illinois after the war.

Daniel put down the diary and took a deep breath. Jake, wandering around the Beaver's edge, came up to Daniel and forced his head under Daniel's hand. Daniel rubbed Jake's head and scratched his ears without much thought about what he was doing. His mind was on Gus. He wondered if Gus made it back to Summertown okay. He wondered if he was able to find his mother and father and if they were still alive. He couldn't imagine having to be away from Emily for forty-six years. Six months were almost unbearable for him.

Suddenly, Jake's ears perked up, and he gave a low growl while looking into the distance. Daniel turned his head and looked in the same direction as the dog. Unfortunately, his night vision wasn't nearly as good as Jake's. Daniel got up from his place at the edge of the porch and slowly moved to the cabin door. He reached inside while still trying to see what Jake was seeing. Leaning next to the open doorway was his rifle. He took the gun in his hands, then reached up, took the powder horn and leather poke containing lead shot, and took them from the peg on the wall where they had been hanging.

He quietly walked down the porch steps and moved away from the house. Daniel walked down toward Beaver Creek in the direction that Jake was looking. He grabbed Jake's collar to keep him from running toward whatever held his attention. Jake's growl grew louder as they moved through the darkness. Daniel slowly and quietly cocked back the hammer of his rifle. Jake began lunging and pulling against Daniel's grip when suddenly, a dark figure stood up on two legs in front of them and let out a mighty roar. Daniel felt the heat of the creature's breath and the wetness of its saliva as the creature spit out its anger like a mouth full of spoiled milk.

It was a black bear. A male that was nearly as tall as Daniel angrily stood on his rear legs before the two of them. In his surprise at seeing the massive, intimidating animal, Daniel lost his grip on Jake's collar. Jake surged toward the bear just as it began its attack on Daniel. It swatted at Daniel with his massive front paw. It missed him but knocked the rifle from his hands. When the cocked gun hit the ground, it fired into the darkness.

Daniel heard one of the horses scream out in pain, and the two mules began to bray seemingly without end.

Jake barked, snarled, and growled as he circled the boar bear, never getting close enough for the bear to reach him. Daniel realized Jake was attempting to keep the bear away from him. It was working. The bear turned his attention toward the dog and away from Daniel. Daniel seized the moment to scramble for his rifle. He reloaded and turned toward the bear, aiming into the darkness. As he pointed the gun at the bear, he hesitated to pull the trigger. Jake and the bear were dancing around in circles, making it difficult for Daniel to fire at the bear without hitting Jake.

Daniel yelled to Jake, "Jake, away!"

Jake scrambled away from the bear, removing himself from the line of fire. Daniel quickly aimed again and pulled the trigger. CLICK. Nothing happened. Daniel checked his rifle. The firing pin evidently bent when the rifle was knocked from his hands. There would be no way to fire the weapon without repair.

The bear turned again on Daniel and lunged at him, roaring like a lion and baring his teeth. Daniel could smell the foulness of the bear's breath. He raised his rifle to swing it at the bear like a club. The bear parried at the movement and knocked the gun from Daniel's grip again. This time, the bear moved against Daniel without determent, even with Jake nipping and grabbing his hindquarters. As the bear came down from his upright position, Daniel raised his left forearm to keep the bear from grabbing his throat as Daniel fell backward, then screamed out in pain.

Now Jake moved to the front of the bear and grabbed him by the ear as the bear held Daniel's arm in his teeth. Jake did everything he could to distract the bear and keep him from ripping Daniel's arm from his body.

Tears began to pour from Daniel's eyes from the extreme pain he felt in his arm. He tried to block out the pain enough to gather his wits. Finally, he remembered the hunting knife hanging from his belt. As the bear continued to rock Daniel's body back and forth, Daniel managed to reach the handle of his knife and slip it from its sheath. His target was an easy one. The bear was right on top of him. He slid the blade under his left forearm and found the bear's throat. He plunged the knife with all his might, sinking it deep into the bear's throat. Daniel then raked the blade in a downward motion, severing the bear's artery. The bear's grip loosened a bit as he began to gurgle on his own blood. Jake continued to tug and pull at the bear's ear until the bear fell away from Daniel's arm.

Through much effort, Daniel managed to roll the four-hundred-pound beast off of him. He was covered in the bear's blood as well as his own. Sweating and gasping for air, Daniel fell backward, lying exhausted on the ground.

Jake whimpered as he approached Daniel and licked him in the face. Daniel dropped the knife from his right hand, then reached up and rubbed Jake's head. "Thanks, buddy!" he said breathily. "You're a good boy!"

CHAPTER 10

May 16, 1819

Emily didn't sleep during the night. She awoke with a restless feeling that something was wrong back home. Emily blearily dragged herself from her mat, which lay on the ground inside her tent. She quickly dressed, combed out her hair, and tied it back before exiting her tent.

A morning breeze wafted across her face as she looked around to see who might be up at such an early hour. She heard a mockingbird just a few feet away, singing her song of endless tunes. Emily looked up, searching for the bird, and was reminded of the mocking-jays from the book ***The Hunger Games***. As she continued to search for the bird, she softly said to herself in her best British accent, "May the odds be ever in your favor."

"What was that you said?" asked Dolly Gordon as she walked up, seemingly out of nowhere.

Startled, Emily jerked as she was wakened from her light trance. "Oh! Nothing.", Emily said. "I was just listening to the birds." Emily looked at Dolly and asked, "How is Captain Gordon this morning? Did he sleep, alright?"

"Yes!" replied Dolly. "He got a good night's sleep and seemed to be in pretty good spirits this morning."

Emily responded, "Well, that's good. I'm afraid I'm going to have to leave today. There doesn't seem to be much I can do for him right now. He's just worn out, and rest is the best medicine for him at this point."

Dolly replied, "Well, Emily, I'm so thankful for all you've done for him. Thank you so much for coming and checking on him."

Emily said, "It has been my pleasure. Please don't hesitate to send for me if you need me for anything."

The two temporarily parted as Dolly went to the cooking area to oversee breakfast. Emily scanned the area, looking for Tommy. She needed to let him know she intended to return home that day. Looking over her left shoulder, she saw him coming out of his tent, still bleary-eyed and yawning from his night's sleep. Emily walked directly to him.

"Mornin', Em'ly," he greeted her.

Very business-like, Emily responded, "Good morning. Tommy, have you spoken to the Gordons yet about you and Amy?"

"Well, naw. Not yet. I just can't seem to come up with the right words to say to 'um."

Emily sighed deeply and said, "Tommy, if you're going to ask, ask this morning. I have to return home today, and I'd like you to go back with me."

Tommy said, "Oh! Well, I guess I'd better get to it then. I'll see to it right after breakfast then."

As everyone gathered to eat their breakfast at the tables, Tommy seemed to be deeply thinking over his eggs and bacon. Amy noticed he wasn't himself and whispered to him as she sat beside him, "Tommy, are you alright?"

"Yeah.", he replied. "Just got a lot on my mind."

Amy asked, "Is there anything I can do to help?"

"Naw.", said Tommy. "I reckon I gotta do this fer m'self."

When breakfast was concluded, and the women began clearing the tables, Tommy looked over to Amy. He said, "Excuse me, Amy. I got somethin' to do." Then Tommy walked away.

Amy watched him with curiosity as he walked toward her mother. She saw them talking but was too far away to hear the conversation.

Tommy asked Dolly, "Ms. Gordon? I wonder if I might have a word with you?"

Suspiciously, Dolly raised one eyebrow and said, "Sure, Mr. Brown. What can I help you with?"

"Well, ma'am, I was wonderin' if we could talk somewhere private?" Dolly paused for a moment and became even more suspicious.

"Sure. Why don't you walk with me for a bit."

The two of them strolled toward the newly built brick house completed only a few months ago. As they cleared the area away from curious ears, Tommy looked around to see if anyone was watching them. "Okay, Mr. Brown. What would you like to talk about?"

"Well, ma'am. I was wonderin', how's Captain Gordon feelin' this mornin'?"

Dolly replied, "He's still very weak. He sleeps most of the time now. Why?"

Tommy cleared his throat and asked, "Well, do you think he might feel good enough to talk to me for a bit?"

"What about?" Dolly asked.

Tommy cleared his throat again and said, "Well, uhm, I was wontin' to ask him if I could marry Amy. But if he ain't feelin' good, is that somethin' I could ask you about instead?"

Dolly stopped suddenly and stared at Tommy briefly before saying, "Well, Mr. Brown, why don't you and I discuss it? I can speak to the captain later. Tell me, Mr. Brown, what did you do before you came here with Emily?"

Tommy replied, "I was a park ranger."

Dolly asked, "And, what does a park ranger do?"

"Well, I mostly patrolled up and down the Natchez Trace, uh I mean road, and made sure everybody obeyed the laws."

Dolly asked, "So you were a lawman?"

"Yes, ma'am," he responded.

"Did you ever arrest anyone?"

Tommy replied, "Well, me and my partner, Ranger Douglas, once arrested these two fellers for possession of an illegal substance. But mostly folks who traveled down the Trace were good people. I might write an occasional speeding ticket, but mostly it was a pretty quiet job."

Dolly thought for a moment, then asked, "What's a speeding ticket?"

"Oh!" said Tommy. "It's a citation we give folks when they're drivin' too fast. They have to pay a fine. Usually, it could be a couple a hundred dollars, dependin' own how fast they're drivin'."

"How fast do people drive?"

Tommy replied," Well, the speed limit is fifty miles per hour. But I pulled a feller over once fer doin' eighty."

Dolly's eyes widened as she exclaimed, "Eighty! I swanny! Excuse my French. How fast can horses run where you come from?"

Tommy smiled a little as he heard her say, "*swanny*." He hadn't heard that word used since his granny used it. "Oh, no ma'am. Horses don't run that fast. People drive automobiles. They're like carriages that don't need a horse to pull 'em. They have a motor that makes them go. Some of them can go more than a hundred miles per hour."

"My, my, my!" Dolly replied. "Well then, what do you plan on doing now that you're here?" she asked.

"Well," Tommy began. "Emily and Daniel have offered me a partnership in their place. I'm going to be a farmer with Daniel. Emily said that if she wanted to, Amy could work with her and learn how to help folks with their ailments."

"So, you're going to be partners with Daniel? You mind if I call Emily over here to verify that?"

Tommy smiled and said, "Oh, no ma'am. I don't mind at all."

Dolly looked around to find Emily. Emily was standing near the tents, trying to look occupied. At the same time, she watched the conversation between Dolly and Tommy from afar. When Dolly got Emily's attention, Dolly beckoned her to come over to them. Emily tried to look innocent as she looked around to see who Dolly might have been motioning to. She then pointed to herself and mouthed the word, "*Me?*" When Dolly nodded her head at Emily, Emily began walking toward the couple.

Dolly asked her, "Emily? Mr. Brown here says that he's been made a full partner in your farm."

Emily smiled and said, "Well, yes. It's true."

Then Dolly said, "He also said you're willing to teach Amy how to doctor folks."

Emily responded, "Well, I won't teach her to be a doctor. I'm not a doctor, I'm only a registered nurse. But I can teach Amy to be a nurse. I'm qualified to do that."

Then Dolly turned to Tommy and asked, "Where will you two live?"

Tommy replied, "Well, Emily said we could build a cabin right there on the farm."

Dolly looked at Emily for a response. Emily nodded her head in agreement.

Dolly looked at Tommy again and asked, "When were you planning on marrying her? You know, she's only fourteen."

Tommy squirmed a bit as he searched for an answer. "Well, she turns fifteen in a few days. Is that too young for her to get married?"

Dolly stared at him as she mulled it over. "She'll turn fifteen on June first. No. It's not too young. It just doesn't give us much time to plan for a wedding. And, with the captain being bedridden, I just don't know."

Emily suddenly realized that time was a problem. If they waited too long, the captain would never see his youngest daughter married. June sixteenth was the day of his death. Emily broke the silence by saying, "May I suggest?"

Dolly looked at her and said, "Sure."

Emily asked, "How long will it take for you to get a preacher here?"

Dolly replied, "We could probably get one here in a week or two."

Emily suggested, "Why don't you send for the preacher and have him come the week after Amy's birthday. That way, each year she can have her birthday and then later have her wedding anniversary, so they won't be on the same day. We'll go back today and see if we can get started on a cabin for the new couple."

"That sounds good, Emily. Mr. Brown, why don't you come back and help her celebrate her birthday on the first, and then we'll have the wedding on Friday the fourth."

Tommy replied, "That sounds just fine, Ms. Gordon, but I wish you would call me Tommy."

Dolly smiled and said, "Of course, and why don't you call me Dolly."

Tommy said, "Sounds good to me. Dolly? Would you mind if I went and said goodbye to Amy before we have to leave?"

Dolly said, "Not at all, Tommy. You can give her the good news while you do."

Tommy nodded in acknowledgment to Dolly and Emily as he turned and walked away. Dolly and Emily watched as Tommy approached Amy, who was still working with the other women cleaning the breakfast dishes. They watched as Tommy walked up to Amy. They watched as Amy dried her hands with the towel slung over her shoulder. They watched as Tommy spoke to her and supposedly told her they would be wed in a few weeks. And then, they watched as Amy wrapped her arms around Tommy excitedly, and the two embraced. Then, Tommy bent down and kissed his bride-to-be.

Emily said, "Tommy is like a little brother to me. You won't have to worry, Dolly. She'll be in good hands. Daniel and I will make sure of it."

Dolly replied, "I know she'll be just fine. I'm worried about what she'll do to that poor young man." They both smiled with tears in their eyes and then chuckled at Dolly's jest.

Chapter II

Emily and Tommy arrived at Beaver Creek mid-afternoon. As they rode their horses through the creek, Emily scanned the area for Daniel. He was nowhere to be found. Instead, Jake came from the cabin's front porch to greet them. Jake whined as they approached, and he wagged his tail so hard that it caused his whole body to bend in half. First to the left, and then to the right.

Emily had a sick feeling in the pit of her stomach. She handed her reins to Tommy and quickly jumped off the back of the mare. She ran into the cabin and found Daniel lying on the bed, his left arm wrapped in a bloody towel. He was sweating profusely and was unconscious.

"Tommy! Come quick!" Emily yelled.

Tommy jumped off the black and ran into the cabin to see what was the matter.

Emily said, "Tommy! Build a fire and start heating some water for me."

Tommy did as she instructed.

Daniel woke at the sound of Emily's yelling.

"Emily?" he whispered.

"Daniel!" she replied. "What happened?"

"Bear attack," he managed to say with a breathy voice. "Last night, I think."

He was burning up with fever. Emily reached for her medical bag and rummaged through it until she found a thermometer. She shook the mercury down until it dropped below the average temperature. Then placed it in Daniel's mouth, under his tongue. While she waited for it to reach maximum temperature, she carefully reached for his left arm. Daniel winced as she began to unwrap the bloody towel carefully. Once she had it uncovered, she saw that the bleeding had slowed but was still flowing. The muscles of his forearm were a mangled mess.

She removed the thermometer from Daniel's mouth and held it to the light to read it. One-hundred, one point five degrees. When she returned to examine his arm, he offered, "I'm pretty sure it's broken. I heard it snap when the bear bit down on it."

Emily said more to herself than to Daniel, "This is going to be tricky. I've got to sew up these lacerations before I can set your arm."

She reached for her bag again and searched for a needle, sutures, and medical clamps. She asked Tommy to grab one of the bottles of rubbing alcohol she had stored on a shelf with all of the other medical supplies that wouldn't fit in her kit. She opened the bottle and poured a generous amount over Daniel's arm, which made Daniel's whole body convulse because of the burning sensation. Blood continued to flow from the open wounds. She prepared her suture and began stitching up the lacerations on his forearm.

After thirty minutes or so, she finished. "Tommy, can you please pour up some of the water that's been heating, into a bowl and bring it to me?"

Tommy did as she requested, never saying a word. She took a clean towel and soaked it in hot water, then began washing away the blood from Daniel's arm. She washed his face and the rest of his exposed body as well.

"Tommy, I need you to find me four splints. Look in the woodpile and find four pieces of wood that are no more than an inch in diameter. Split them if you have to. I need four that are all about the same length. No more than twelve inches long."

Tommy nodded and ran outside to find what she needed. Emily took a dry, clean towel and dried the moisture from Daniel's wounded arm. She went to the storage shelves and grabbed some gauze bandages. When Tommy came back into the cabin, he handed Emily four thin sticks of wood. She took them and measured them against the length of Daniel's forearm.

"That's perfect!" she said. "Now, Tommy, I need you to raise Daniel up off the bed so that he is sitting up."

Tommy did as he was told. "Now, sit on the bed behind him and hold him upright. That's it. Now wrap your arms around his body, including his upper arms. I need you to hold him steady while I set these broken bones."

While Tommy braced himself against Daniel, Emily took a small towel and raised it to Daniel's mouth. "Here, bite down on this. This is really going to hurt."

As Daniel bit down on the towel, his body tensed. Tommy increased his grip around Daniel's body. Emily gripped Daniel's wrists with both her hands and readied herself to pull against Tommy's hold. When she was satisfied Daniel's arm was in the right position, she said, "On the count of three. One ..."

Emily pulled with all of her might. "Aah!" Daniel gave a muffled scream. Then it was over.

Emily wrapped Daniel's wounded arm in gauze and placed the splints on it, holding them in place with more of the dressing. She would need to change the bandages periodically, so putting Daniel's arm in a cast was out of the question. Emily then told Daniel to lie back on the bed. She added some peppermint oil to a pan of water. She soaked a washcloth in the water and oil mixture, then bathed Daniel with it to help bring down his fever.

"Okay, tell me what happened," she said to him.

With a heavy breath, Daniel explained the incident of last night's events. He then said, "Tommy? Can you go check on the horses? I think I may have accidentally shot one of them."

Tommy nodded and exited the cabin. He decided to put up Emily's mare and the black that Tommy had been riding while he checked on the others. Tommy led the two horses through the gate, then unsaddled them. He walked around the corral, checking on the two mules and the other three horses. None of them appeared to be limping as they avoided him. Then, he thought he spotted something on the colt. He was a little over a year old now. Tommy got closer. There it was. On the left hind quarter of the yearling colt was a slight gash, about three inches long. It had been bleeding at one point but had stopped.

Tommy threw a lasso over the yearling's head and led him toward the gate, where he tied him to a post. He then went into the cabin to make a report to Daniel. "Looks like you might've clipped the colt with that stray shot. He's got a small gash, but it's not bleedin' none."

Emily reached into her medical kit and brought out a bottle of iodine and a cotton ball. "Here," she said. "Clean the wound with this. He should be fine."

Tommy took the bottle and cotton ball from Emily and then returned to the corral. He entered the corral again and moved over to the colt. He pushed the young horse up against the fence wall so the wound was exposed, but the colt couldn't retreat from him. He poured some of the iodine onto the cotton ball and dabbed it onto the colt's rump. The young horse pawed at the ground with disdain, then swished his tail into Tommy's face. In disgust, Tommy spat the coarse horsehair from his mouth and grumpily said, "Hold own thar, you punk! I"m jest tryin' to hep ya!"

The colt pawed at the ground again and nodded several times to warn Tommy to leave him alone. Satisfied that the wound had been well treated, Tommy stood and said to the colt, "Alright, you scruff! That art ta do ya!"

Tommy untied the yearling and watched him canter away to join the other animals.

Tommy went back into the cabin and handed Emily the bottle of iodine. As he did, Daniel said to him, "I hear you're about to become a married man. Congratulations!"

Tommy blushed a little and responded, "Thanks. I'll go check on the other animals and make sure they're all fed." He then turned and left the cabin.

Daniel looked at Emily and asked, "Did I say something wrong?"

Emily replied, "No, he's just a little uncomfortable about the whole thing. He wants to marry Amy, but I think he's a little embarrassed about their age difference."

Daniel asked, "Well, when is the wedding?"

Emily answered, "June fifth."

Daniel raised his brow and asked, "That's mighty soon, isn't it?"

Emily responded, "Amy turns fifteen on the first, and Dolly thought she should be at least fifteen before Amy wed. I suggested that date because I knew Captain Gordon wouldn't last much longer. He will at least be there to see his youngest daughter married." Daniel nodded in agreement, then decided to lie back down to rest.

Once outside, Tommy realized that buzzards had begun occupying the valley's skies. No doubt, they had smelled the scent of blood in the area and searched for their next victim, he thought. So, after checking the livestock and gathering eggs, he took out his knife and began skinning the bear that still lay on the ground close to Beaver Creek. The meat would not be useful at this point. It had been appropriately bled with Daniel's cut to the throat.

However, it had been lying in the hot sun of the late Spring for more than a day. It would likely be tainted now. The hide, on the other hand, would be useful. He took his time and carefully removed the skin from the gigantic carcass that lay before him. At times, it was challenging to roll the massive creature over so that he could continue his delicate slicing away the skin from meat and bone. It had been nearly an hour before he had finished. He then took a hatchet and swung it down into the animal's skull, cracking it open. He removed the brain from the head and placed it in a large clay jar along with some water. It would be used later to tan the hide. Then he looked at the massive claws protruding from the bear's paws. He decided to remove them. He used his tomahawk to extract the claws, then placed them in his haversack. He would present them to Daniel later.

Tommy dragged the bearskin down to the creek and thoroughly washed it. He didn't have time to prepare the tanning paste right away, so he looked around for something to store the hide in until he could work on it. Tommy spotted a crate from his and Emily's trip through the Shimmering that would be just the right size. He carried the container over to the creek bed, placed the hide into it, and lowered it into the water to keep the fur from drying out before he could tan it.

He then collected his horse from the corral. Tommy tied a rope around the bear's carcass and dragged it to the valley's far end, where buzzards or other scavengers could consume it.

CHAPTER 12

May 24, 1819:

The bright, orange sun rose above the treetops in the eastern sky above the Water Valley. Bleary-eyed, Tommy dragged himself from his bedroll and stumbled out of the tent. He looked around for any sign of life besides himself. No one was stirring outside. The horses and mules were moving around in the corral, anxiously waiting to be fed.

Tommy got busy tending to the livestock and making sure everyone was fed. He gathered eggs from the nesting boxes, fighting off pecks from the hens who attempted to protect their prized possessions from this would-be thief. Tommy took the eggs to the cabin and found the door open. He poked his head through the doorway and said, "Mornin'!".

"Good morning, Tommy!" Emily replied.

Tommy stepped inside, finding Daniel and two young men sitting at the table. Two of the Gordon boys arrived the evening before, just before dark. Dolly Gordon had decided that two men and a woman would not be enough to raise a cabin in time for Amy and Tommy's wedding day. So, she sent Luke and James to assist. Little did she know that Daniel was of little help because of a broken arm. They were all very excited and thankful to see the Gordon boys ride into the valley.

Tommy handed Emily the eggs. "Thank you, Tommy!" she said as she placed them in a bowl sitting on a countertop. "Have a seat!".

Tommy joined the other men already consuming large helpings of scrambled eggs, bacon, and biscuits.

After breakfast, the men exited the cabin to begin their work on Tommy and Amy's cottage. Emily stayed to clear the table and clean the breakfast dishes. Jake lingered behind, waiting to see what might fall to the floor. Emily saw him out of the corner of her eye and looked around to see what might be available. There, on the table, lay one biscuit. She picked it up and handed it to Jake, who took it and held it in his mouth. Jake remained, looking up at Emily with sad eyes. "Sorry, Jake!" she said. "No bacon today. The men ate it all". Jake solemnly turned and left the cabin to sit in the sun and enjoy his biscuit in solitude.

Tommy and Luke hitched the two mules to their harnesses while Daniel and James gathered the tools they needed for the day. Logs that had been left from the building of the first cabin would need to be dragged to the new build site. Tommy's cabin was being built at the other end of the Water Valley, about a quarter of a mile away. It would be within sight of the first cabin but still provided a degree of privacy for each couple. They would have plenty of fresh water, as the cabin would sit near Beaver Creek, just as Daniel and Emily's home did. Between the two cabins lay seventy-five acres of corn and ten acres of pasture. At the back of the property, circling the valley, was about one hundred acres of timber.

Over the past six days, Tommy, Emily, and Daniel had managed to construct the foundation and stack the first run of logs. It had been slow work because of Daniel's injury. He couldn't do much to help other than leading one of the mules. They only had seven days to finish the cabin building before Tommy had to leave to return to the Gordon House. Tommy had promised to be back for Amy's fifteenth birthday on June 1st, and then they would wed on the fourth.

With the extra hands, they made good progress. Daniel and Emily worked together, hauling logs to the building site. James used the other mule to raise the logs to their proper position along the walls while Tommy and Luke secured the logs, notching them into place.

By the end of May 27th, they had completed the house's walls. On the 28th, they began building the chimney and fireplace and began chinking the walls. On the 30th, they finished the roof shingles. By noon on the 31st, they had hung the door and the window shutters.

Amy would now have a place to call home. Although not nearly as extravagant as the house her parents now lived in or both her sisters' homes back in Nashville, it would be hers and Tommy's to share. It would be a place for them to grow their love for one another and start a family.

After their noon meal, Tommy and the Gordon boys walked down to the Beaver and bathed before they left to travel to the Gordon place. Emily and Daniel would join them on June 4th.

Once the three men had left, Emily cleaned the cabin, preparing for Amy's arrival. Daniel couldn't help, so he sat down and read from Gus's diary.

August 7, 1774

I feel lucky to be alive. In the early morning after my birthday, I went outside to pee. I was attacked by a mountain lion. I thought I would die. Thankfully, Timothy heard the commotion and came to the rescue. He shot the cat before it could do too much damage. I ended up with several deep scratches on my stomach and arms. I was sore the next day from that heavy cat landing on me, but I'm doing ok now.

Daniel sat and pondered for a moment. "Wow!" he thought to himself. "Gus never told me a cougar had attacked him.

August 5, 1774

Gus awoke with a start. It was early in the morning and still dark. His dream of being captured by Indians had awakened him. It was the same dream as before. This time, they had him tied down on the ground, spread eagle, and tied to stakes so that he could not move. The Indians were questioning him, but he couldn't understand them. They threatened him with a knife placed at his throat. He did understand the threat but didn't know why they were threatening him or what they wanted.

When he awoke, he was panting and sweating. He felt his wrists to see if his bindings were still there. They were not. He carefully tried to lift his head. It was not a problem. He was no longer in danger of death. The Indians were nowhere to be found inside the cave where he and Timothy had been sleeping.

"*Why am I having the same dream over and over*?" he wondered. He had not seen any Indians in the area since Timothy had found him. Was it because of the experience of seeing his friend Robbie executed by the savages? He wished he could forget it. He missed Robbie and his mom and dad. He ached so badly to be home in his own bed at the Grove.

He decided to get up and go outside. He walked over to the nearest tree and relieved his bladder. There was a slight mist in the air. When finished, he fastened up his britches and prepared to walk back into the cave. As he turned away from the tree, he heard a low growl not too far away. He froze. He slowly scanned the area, searching for a clue about what he had heard. His heart began to beat rapidly in his chest. He couldn't tell from which direction the growl had come. He slowly turned to look behind him.

He scanned the area again. He still couldn't see anything, but the noise persisted.

The hair on the back of his neck began to rise as if a magnet was pulling against it. He decided to look up. There it was. About sixteen feet above him, resting on a branch of an Elm tree, was a pair of green eyes. Gus gasped for air, searching and reaching for the courage to not turn and run. He slowly moved toward the cave, not turning on the unknown creature that hovered over him.

Suddenly, Gus heard a scream. It sounded like a terrified woman. *"Did that sound come from me?"* he wondered. As he stared at the eyes watching him, he began to make out a silhouette, and his eyes adjusted to the darkness. When he realized what it was, it was too late.

The cougar let out another scream as it leaped from the branch, aiming for Gus. Gus instinctively raised both of his arms to guard against the attack. He heard himself cry out as the cat landed on him, knocking him to the ground. Although Gus had been knocked to the ground, he managed to push the big cat off of him. When Gus rolled back to his feet, he found himself face-to-face with the angry feline.

The cougar continued to growl and scream at Gus as they circled one another in the darkness. Gus glanced around continuously, searching for something he could use as a weapon. A piece of firewood or a rock. Why had he not brought his spear out with him, or his rifle, or even a knife? Gus realized that he was hurting. Both of his arms were burning with pain. He could feel the blood starting to drip from his hand onto the ground.

Gus decided to back up toward the cave. If he got close enough, he might be able to wake Timothy. He backed slowly from the cat, trying very hard not to lose his footing. The cougar followed, matching him step for step as it pursued Gus. The lion continued with his growls and screams as if trying to intimidate Gus. It was working.

Gus managed to back away from the cat at about twenty paces when suddenly he tripped on a tree root, causing him to fall backward and land hard on his backside. The cougar seized its opportunity, lunging for Gus from eight feet away. Again, Gus raised his arms to protect himself from the attack and braced for impact. A shot rang out from behind Gus as he felt the cat's weight hit his body, causing him to grunt as if the breath had been knocked out of him. Gus waited for the cat's teeth to dig into his skin or claws to be raking his torso. But neither happened. The cougar just lay there on top of him, lifeless.

Gus closed his eyes and lay on the ground without moving, the cougar resting on top of him. Then he heard footsteps from behind him.

"Are you dead?" It was Timothy.

"I think I'm still alive," said Gus.

Timothy reached out with his free hand while holding his smoking rifle in his other. Gus accepted his hand as Timothy pulled Gus up off of the ground. The cougar rolled off of Gus as he was lifted.

"Are you hurt?" asked Timothy.

"Yeah, I'm pretty sure I am. My hands feel sticky from blood," replied Gus.

"Well, let's get you inside and take a look, then."

Timothy grabbed Gus's left arm to steady Gus as they shuffled together back into the cave.

Chapter 13

June 4, 1819

Daniel and Emily arose before daybreak. They had much to do before making the half-day ride to the Gordon place. Emily packed up their things and placed them into saddlebags. They would need a change of clothes for the wedding, food for the short trip and a gift for the bride and groom. Daniel would see to the animals before they left. He made sure they all had access to plenty of food and water. They planned to be gone only for one day, but he wanted to make sure they had plenty in case something delayed their return.

Daniel saddled Hoss and the blue-eyed sorrel. They would leave the mare behind because she was pregnant again. As Daniel led the horses up to the cabin, Emily exited the cabin carrying two sets of saddlebags, both filled to overflowing. Daniel looked at her and chuckled a little as he said, "Always prepared, aren't you."

Without cracking a smile, Emily responded, "Always!"

She swung the saddlebags up over the backs of each of the saddles and tied them down. Then she moved back to the cabin. "What ja forget? The kitchen sink?" asked Daniel.

Emily reached inside the cabin door without entering the cabin. She brought out two powder horns, two braces and pistols, and two rifles. Emily slung one of the braces over her shoulder along with a powder horn. She offered the others to Daniel. "I don't think I can wear that thing with this sling." She took the brace back and slung it over her other shoulder.

Then strapped a rifle to each of the saddles. She then mounted the sorrel and waited for Daniel.

Daniel saw that she was in a determined mood this morning. He thought he'd better not challenge her. Once he mounted Hoss, he said, "Wait, let me have one of those pistols. I can carry it in my sling."

Emily reached into one of the braces, pulled out one of the pistols, and handed it to Daniel. "Here! You can have the little one!"

They turned their horses, walked them through Beaver Creek, and headed northwest toward the Gordon place. The sun barely peeked above the hillside surrounding the Water Valley. The birds were already stirring and singing their morning songs. The sweet aroma of honeysuckle filled the air as they passed by the blooms that clung to their vines. The squirrels could be heard chattering as they chased one another through the treetops. It was the perfect morning for a ride.

Jake led the way as they walked their horses down the trail that led to the Gordon house. About an hour down the path, Daniel noticed Jake as he froze in his tracks. Jake lifted his nose to the air and sniffed while letting out a muffled "*woof.*"

Daniel pulled up and motioned for Emily to do the same. He felt Hoss's body tense beneath his own. Hoss pricked up his ears toward something that Daniel couldn't see. "What is it?" Emily whispered.

Daniel shook his head in response to her question without looking at her.

Suddenly, Jake began to growl deep in his throat. Then, his growl turned to a ferocious barking as a man appeared on the trail from behind a hackberry tree. He was average height, clean-shaven, wearing a frock coat and a three-cornered hat. "Mornin', folks.", he spoke while aiming a pistol in his right hand toward Daniel.

Jake's barking continued until Daniel yelled, "Jake! Down!"

Jake yielded without taking his eyes off the man. He continued to growl in a low tone.

"What do you want, mister?" asked Daniel.

"Well, it ain't what I want. It's what I need. I need your horses. Mine got shot out from under me a couple a days back by some injuns. I managed to git away on foot, but seems like my luck might've just changed."

Daniel said, "I wouldn't be too sure about that, mister."

The stranger looked at Daniel with curiosity and responded, "Seems to me you're a might stove up. I don't think I've got too much to worry about with you. Now sister here, she's armed to the teeth. But she also shows fear in her eyes. I think I'll be just fine. Miss, how 'bout you real easy like, drop them pistols down on the ground, here in front of me."

Emily eased her pistol from its brace and tossed it toward the stranger.

"That's good. Now, pull that rifle of yours and drop it down here too."

Emily complied. "Good. Now do the same with your man's rifle. Drop it down here."

Emily did as she was told. "Alright, now. Here's where it gets tricky. Ya'll step down from them horses real slow and don't make any sudden moves."

As they began to dismount, Daniel whispered to Emily, "Keep the horse in front of you."

As Daniel slid off Hoss's left side, he reached into his sling with his right hand and gripped the pistol he had been hiding. Daniel yelled, "Jake!" as his right foot touched the ground.

Jake suddenly lunged at the man, startling him as he did. The stranger raised his pistol and aimed it at Jake, but before he could pull the trigger, Daniel fired his gun, hitting the man in his right eye. Blood, bone, flesh, and hair exploded from the back of the stranger's head. The stranger's grip tightened on the trigger, causing his own gun to fire. The projectile whizzed past Emily's head, barely missing her.

Daniel, startled by the second shot, quickly turned to find Emily. "Are you okay?" he asked.

She stared back at him with wide eyes and said, "I think so."

Emily looked over the back of her horse to see what happened to the stranger.

"Is he dead?" she asked.

"Yeah, I'm pretty sure he is," said Daniel.

Daniel walked over to examine the stranger's body. He placed his pistol back inside the sling and drew his knife from its sheath. He nudged the body that lay before him with his foot. It didn't move. Daniel knelt down and placed two of his fingers across the man's neck to feel for a pulse. "He's dead!" he called out to Emily.

Emily walked over to join Daniel by the stranger's side. "Well, what do we do with the body?" she asked.

Daniel replied, "I guess we'll load him onto the back of your horse, and you'll have to ride double with me."

Emily said, "Dolly's gonna love you. How many will this be?"

Daniel replied, "This is the third body. But only the first one that I killed. If you recall, the Black Hand killed the other two."

Emily said, "You're getting pretty good with these weapons."

"Emily, I didn't want to kill him. It was him or us, and I wasn't going to give him our horses."

Emily replied, "Oh, I'm not complaining, Daniel. I'm just admiring how well David Colbert taught you. Now, if we can just get him to teach you to quit feeding the bears."

Daniel smiled, then chuckled at her joke. Then, the two of them loaded the stranger's body onto the back of the sorrel. Once the corpse was tied down to the saddle, Daniel mounted Hoss. He then removed his left foot from the stirrup to allow Emily to climb up onto the back of the horse behind him. Emily wrapped her arms around Daniel as they continued down the trail.

Three hours later and just before noon, they rode into the Gordon place, having made the journey without further incident. Dolly Gordon, Amy, and Tommy Brown all came to meet them as they rode into the camp area. Dolly's smile turned to a look of concern when she noticed the body strapped to the sorrel's back.

"Well, Daniel," she began to speak. "You know you don't have to bring in a dead body every time you come to see me."

With a sheepish look on his face, Daniel replied, "Sorry, Dolly. This fellow thought he would relieve us of our horses. I let him know differently."

Dolly said, "Well, step down, then. I'll have Titas take care of it."

As they stepped down from the horse, Daniel handed the reins of both horses to a black man named Homer, who approached them and greeted them. "Good day, Suh. Mam. Can I take care of yo hosses fo yuh?"

Daniel replied, "Thank you, Homer."

Daniel and Emily looked around and noticed that the camp had increased the number of tents. Many people had arrived for the wedding. Dolly introduced them to the rest of her family. Her daughter, Belinda James, was married to an attorney in Nashville named Westbrook. They had a two-year-old daughter named Kelly. Another of Dolly's daughters, Cynthia, was married to the owner of a whiskey distillery. His name was Trevor Allen. Then they met Lucy. Lucy was not yet married but spent much of her time in Nashville visiting her sisters while prowling for a husband. Many other friends of the Gordons came for the special event.

Emily asked Dolly, "What time will the wedding take place?"

Dolly replied, "Well, we'll have a feast starting around noon. The ceremony will be around three, then we'll celebrate well after dark. I saved you two a tent. It's right over there."

She pointed at a tent near the camp's outer area. "Wonderful.", said Emily. "I think I'd like to freshen up before the feast."

Emily and Daniel went into the tent, washed off the dust from their trail ride, and then changed into more appropriate clothing.

When Emily and Daniel exited their tent, it was nearly noon. Emily carried the gift that she and Daniel planned to present to the young couple. As they looked around, they saw that everyone was beginning to gather around the banquet tables.

Daniel and Emily joined them. In the center of the gathering, they saw Tommy and Amy standing next to Dolly and Captain Gordon. Daniel and Emily were a little surprised to see Captain Gordon on his feet. He was, however, not very steady. He looked exhausted, and it seemed he might topple over at any second.

Dolly raised her hands to get everyone's attention. As the crowd quieted, she said loudly, "Captain Gordon and I want to thank all of you for joining us on this auspicious occasion. I especially want to thank Reverend Emit Crosby for coming all the way from Nashville to perform the wedding ceremony for Tommy and Amy. We also have Jethro Ames and his fellow musicians, who will be performing throughout the celebration. I will ask Reverend Crosby to bless our food, then you may begin to serve yourselves from the banquet tables."

The reverend led everyone in a very long prayer. Most everyone became a little fidgety as the preacher droned on and on. Children could be heard asking their mothers, "When are we going to eat?"

After what seemed to be ten or fifteen minutes, the reverend ended his sermon of a prayer with, "Amen!" Everyone in the congregation enthusiastically (*some sarcastically*) repeated, "Amen!"

Everyone convened around the banquet tables, serving themselves from the platters filled with various foods. There was baked ham, roasted turkey, potatoes, squash, corn on the cob, green beans, field peas, biscuits, and cornbread. The items went on and on.

Rather than filing into line at the banquet tables, Emily and Daniel chose to seek Tommy and Amy. The two of them were standing over to the side at one end of the banquet tables. They were engaged with different groups of people in short congratulatory conversations. When Emily and Daniel finally reached the couple, Tommy and Amy both greeted them with enthusiastic greetings and hugs. Tommy said, "I'm glad you two made it. Did you have any trouble?"

Emily replied, "Oh, you know, Daniel. If there's trouble about, he'll find it."

Tommy looked at Daniel questioningly. "We had a run-in with a stranger about three hours back on the trail. He wanted to relieve us of our horses," Daniel offered.

Then, Tommy asked, "And?"

"I changed his mind for him," Daniel replied.

Emily spoke to Amy, "I see your father is up and about. Is he feeling well?"

Amy said, "He's still weak, but he said he wanted to be as much a part of the celebration as possible. Mother and I intend for him to rest a bit this afternoon before the evening celebration. Hopefully, he can hang on long enough to give me away during the ceremony."

Emily offered, "I'm sure he'll be fine. At least I hope so for your sake."

As someone approached and drew Amy's attention away from the Lanes, Tommy spoke to them in a low voice, "Please don't mention the cabin to Amy. Her brothers and I decided a while back to surprise her. She thinks we'll be living in a tent for the next few months."

Emily and Daniel both smiled at the idea of Amy riding into the valley and catching her first glimpse of a new cabin built for her.

When Amy turned back to the Lanes, Emily handed her the gift. "Here," she said "Daniel and I want you to have this as you begin your new lives together as husband and wife."

Tommy moved closer to Amy so he could see better as she opened the gift. Emily had wrapped it in a piece of cloth and tied it with ribbon. Amy excitedly opened the gift and found a small but heavy leather poke inside. Amy opened the poke and poured its contents into her free hand. Several gold coins spilled into her hand. There were so many she nearly dropped them to the ground. Tommy reached out and caught them as they overflowed into Amy's tiny hand. Tommy and Amy were dumbfounded.

Amy said, "Oh, Emily! Daniel! You shouldn't have! Thank you so much!"

Tommy asked, "What's this for?"

Daniel answered, "We thought a young couple starting out could use some cash to get their household started. It's a hundred dollars. I hope it will be enough to help you start your new life together."

Amy and Tommy stared at the coins, nearly in tears. Tommy finally managed to choke away the tears as he said, "This is mighty generous of you. We sure do appreciate it."

After several hours of eating, drinking, and conversation, the congregation of people was called together so that the reverend could perform the ceremony. All were quiet as Amy and Tommy came together and stood with the preacher in front of the crowd. Reverend Crosby was as longwinded at preaching the ceremony as he had been for the prayer of blessing for the meal. Daniel could tell that the man loved to hear himself speak. Crosby was either unaware that the crowd was growing weary of his words or didn't care.

Finally, after thirty minutes or so of telling everyone how sacred marriage is and how the promises of marriage were not to be taken lightly, he began the vows. Amy and Tommy pledged their love to one another in the congregation's presence; then Reverend Crosby pronounced them to be wed. Tommy embraced Amy and kissed her as the crowd erupted in cheer and merriment.

After a couple of hours of more celebration, people slowly began retiring to their beds. Daniel and Emily retired earlier than most. They both knew they would need to get an early start in the morning to get back and tend to their livestock.

Tommy and Amy were among the last to enter their tent. Amy's family had prepared their sleeping quarters, making a pallet on the floor with a feather mattress covered with several quilts and blankets. Amy was not shy as she disrobed and lay on the bed. She watched Tommy as he began to undress. "What are those?" she asked, pointing at Tommy's underwear.

With flushed cheeks, Tommy responded, "Them is boxer briefs."

Amy asked, "Is that what men wear in your world? In the future, I mean?"

Tommy replied, "Some do. Some wear just plain boxers, and some wear briefs. Briefs are shorter than these are."

"Hmm.", said Amy. "I've only seen men in long johns. Like my brothers wear. Those are cute!"

Tommy grew more embarrassed by her remark. "Are you teasin' me, Amy?"

Amy responded, "Why yes, I am, Tommy. Why don't you come to bed and I'll tease you some more?"

Tommy joined her on the pallet. The two embraced passionately until they finally fell asleep in each other's arms.

Chapter 14

June 5, 1819

Emily and Daniel rode back toward the Water Valley just after dawn. The farther down the trail they rode, Emily noticed a sound in the trees. "Do you hear that?" she asked.

Daniel looked around and nodded. "Those are cicadas. It sounds like we might have an outbreak," Emily said a little louder.

As they rode on, Daniel asked, "Will they hurt the crops?"

Emily replied, shaking her head, "No. They are sap eaters. They might damage some of the trees, mostly oak trees. But the corn and the garden crops should be okay."

By the time they entered the valley, the male cicadas' song was deafening to Daniel and Emily's ears. Several times, cicadas would swarm past them annoyingly as they rode toward the cabin. Some ended up in Emily's hair, which she tried to rake out with her fingers. As they rode through Beaver Creek, they noticed the water churning furiously. Some of the cicadas had mistakenly landed on top of the water, and the fish were feasting on them. Emily pointed and said, "Looks like we'll have some nice fat fish."

Daniel grinned and nodded to her.

It was nearly noon when they rode up to the cabin and stopped at the hitching rail in front. The singing was so loud that Daniel and Emily had to yell to one another to be heard as they spoke. Daniel said, "I'll take care of the horses!"

Emily nodded her response. Jake decided to take shelter with Emily as he followed her into the cabin. Jake wasn't fond of the buzzy little creatures that were continually landing on him. He sought refuge under the table but was already covered with the crawling, buzzing, annoying insects. Emily looked at Jake with sympathy and said, "Awe, Jake. Come here and let me get those things off of you."

Jake whimpered to her and slowly crawled from beneath the table. Emily carefully removed each bug from Jake's yellow coat and tossed them out the door. Jake panted and wagged his tail in approval and thanks.

Emily realized she was getting hungry. She looked around the cabin and found a large woven reed basket on the floor beside the shelves. She snatched it up and headed for the door. As she started to open the door, she looked around at Jake and asked, "Are you coming, or are you staying?"

Jake crawled under the table and lay on the floor to tell her he wasn't going anywhere. "Suit yourself."

Emily quickly opened the door and darted out, closing it behind her, trying not to allow more insects to enter the cabin. She made her way toward the back, moving to the garden. Emily intended to gather fresh vegetables for their lunch. She met Daniel on her way, who had just finished caring for the horses and mules. Daniel was making his way toward the rest of the livestock. She smiled at him, grabbed his hand, and asked, "Is this the simpler life you wished for?"

Daniel replied with an even bigger smile, "It is. And I'm going to..."

Emily finished it with him, "Live it to the fullest."

The two parted ways as Emily reached her destination. Daniel continued toward the pens that held the pigs, goats, and chickens. He fed them all, gathered eggs, and then milked the nanny.

Emily walked down the rows of her garden, searching for ripened veggies she could prepare for a quick lunch. She grabbed two tomatoes: okra, yellow squash, and cucumbers. These and some bacon would make a tasty lunch for the two of them. She built a fire outside to fry the bacon. It was too hot in the summer to cook anything indoors.

After lunch, Daniel decided to check on the corn. Emily had already told him that the cicadas weren't after the corn, but he still wanted to check on it. He went to the cornfield and started walking down the first row. She was right, of course. The cicadas weren't eating the corn. However, Daniel found worms crawling around on several of the stalks. He knew they would quickly damage the crop if he didn't do something.

He walked back to the cabin and met Emily just as she finished the clean-up from their lunch. "We've got a problem."

Emily looked concerned and asked, "Its not the cicadas?"

"No.," said Daniel. "Cutworms!"

Emily asked, "What should we do?"

"Well, it will be tedious work, but we need to go worm picking."

Emily said, "Ugh! That sounds wonderful."

"Oh, come on!" said Daniel.

"It won't be as bad as some of the stuff you had to clean up at the hospital."

Emily couldn't argue with him there.

They each found a bucket and then headed toward the cornfield. When Emily and Daniel reached the first row, Daniel instructed, "It will be a lot of walking, but I think we can get a better look at our quarry if we each take a side of the same row. That way, we can see both sides of the stalk."

Emily nodded her approval.

The silks on the corn were light green, which meant the corn was forming inside the shucks but not yet ripe. When the silks turned dark brown or almost black, the corn would be ready to eat. Most of this crop was meant for the livestock to ensure they had plenty to eat over the next winter.

So, the corn would remain on the stalks until it dried. Then, it would be harvested and stored in a corn crib that had not yet been built.

Daniel found it a little inconvenient to carry his bucket with his arm still in a sling. He decided to hang the bucket handle from his broken arm at the elbow and put the sling back around his neck to carry the weight.

They had seventy-five acres to cover. Luckily, the temperature wasn't too unbearable. About eighty degrees, Daniel guessed. They worked steadily, allowing the singing of the cicadas to create a rhythm for them as they picked the one-inch larvae from the corn stalks. Most of the time, the worms had already infiltrated the corn husk at the top of the ear. They carefully opened the husks at the top to expose the unwanted predator, then ripped it from its feeding place.

Some of the hens went to the cornfield from the coop area. Eventually, all of them found their way down. Something told them that there was something worth checking out down there. They scratched around in the dirt, pecking at something only they could see. Occasionally, Daniel would drop a worm to the ground and watch as the fowl dart over instantly to grab the prey.

Daniel said, "Hey, we might not need these buckets after all."

Eventually, the hens had eaten their fill of the larvae, and they wandered off in search of other delicacies.

Emily and Daniel managed to cover around twelve or thirteen acres by dusk. Their backs ached. Their joints were stiff. Their buckets were nearly full. Emily asked, "What should we do with these?"

Daniel said, "Yeah, I've been thinking about that. Why don't we take them down to the Beaver and dump them in the water?"

So, they did. Daniel and Emily carried their buckets to the edge of Beaver Creek. Emily took each bucket one at a time, turning it upside down and spilling its contents into the water. Within seconds, the creek began to churn with energy from below. Fishtails flapped out of the water's surface as perch, trout, and catfish all ascended to eat the worms. Emily and Daniel found it to be quite entertaining.

When they reached the cabin, Jake was very excited to see them. He ran circles around them as they tried to enter. They were both too tired to cook, so they ate a cold meal of leftover vegetables from lunch and some deer jerky.

After they finished cleaning the kitchen, they washed up and got into bed. Daniel and Emily were exhausted. While lying in bed, they reflected on the day's events. Emily asked, "What can we do next year to prevent the cutworms from coming back?"

Daniel replied, "Well, I think the best thing would be to plow the fields in the winter. That will expose the larvae that are hiding underground. The chickens and other birds will eat them after they are exposed. That should keep us from spending so much time picking worms off the stalks next summer.

Emily coyly said, "Well, at least we'll have some help in the future to do the worm picking."

Daniel replied, "Yeah, we sure could have used Tommy and Amy's help today. We would have gotten a lot more accomplished."

Emily chuckled as she said, "Not them, silly! Our children!"

Daniel replied, "Well, yeah. Someday we'll have some kids to . . . wait . . . are you saying you're. . . how far along are you?"

Emily replied, "About three months."

"Three months! Are you crazy! Why did you let me work you so hard today? You might have hurt yourself or the baby!"

Emily said, "Daniel, I'm fine! It was good for me. Its good exercise. Besides, I'm a pioneer woman now. I can't take a six-month vacation. I've got work to do, same as you. Hey, Ree Drummond's got nothing on this chick!"

They both chuckled at her joke. When they finally fell quiet, they drifted off to sleep quickly.

The next day, they woke at dawn to the sunlight peeking through the window. Jake stirred a little and gave a *"woof*!" letting them know he wanted out. Emily crawled out of bed carefully. Her back was sore, and her joints ached, but she reached the door. When she opened the door, Jake darted out, making his rounds, sniffing the area, searching for who knows what. Emily stood in the doorway, enjoying the morning air, watching the sun as it rose above the treetops in the valley. Eventually, Daniel managed to get himself out of bed to join Emily. He stood behind her, wrapping his uninjured arm around her waist. Daniel then used his hand to find her abdomen. He moved his hand in a circular motion, searching for the baby that rested within her. "How long before it starts kicking?"

Emily said, "Not long."

"Listen!" said Daniel. "The cicadas aren't singing as much, now. Have they gone?"

Emily replied, "Most likely, they have moved on. The singing is their mating call. They mated yesterday, the females will lay their eggs in the ground, and at some point they will shed their exoskeletons and move on."

Daniel asked, "Will they be back next year?"

"No," said Emily. "At least not this group. This group or their offspring anyway, won't be back for another thirteen or seventeen years. It depends on the species, and I don't know what kind we had here."

Daniel said, "Thirteen years to reach maturity?"

"Yeah, well, it's not so different from humans. Only we don't spend our first thirteen years underground. You remember we had a group move through a couple of years ago. Well, not from now, but our old time, well, you know what I mean."

Daniel said, "Oh yeah! I remember they were constantly flying through the windows of my mail truck."

"Well," said Daniel. "We better get a move on."

They both got dressed and set about completing their morning chores before moving on to the task they had begun the day before.

They ate a quick breakfast and then went to the cornfield to begin the day's work. The chickens fell behind them as they walked down the rows, picking up whatever Emily or Daniel would drop in their wake. The morning breeze made it a little easier to bear the work. However, the sun was beating down on them by noon like a bass drum.

They took a break and walked back to the cabin for lunch. As Emily and Daniel neared the cabin, they saw two riders coming down the trail toward the creek. It was Tommy and Amy. Emily waved in their direction, and Amy and Tommy both waved back.

When they reached the cabin, they all enthusiastically greeted one another. "Welcome home!" said Emily. "Step down from there and come inside. We were just getting ready to have some lunch."

"Before we all go inside, Tommy, would you mind helping Daniel dump these buckets in the creek. He's still not able to use that bum arm yet."

Tommy said, "Sure, Emily! What's in them, anyway?"

"Cutworms!" exclaimed Daniel. "Seems we have an infestation on our hands."

Tommy asked, "In the corn?"

"Yep!" replied Daniel.

Daniel and Tommy moved to the creek bank while Amy and Emily entered the cabin to prepare lunch. Tommy asked, "So, ya'll been pickin' worms off the corn this mornin'?"

Daniel replied, "This morning and yesterday afternoon. We've managed to get close to twenty acres done. If you and Amy don't mind pitchin' in, we can probably finish up by nightfall tomorrow."

Tommy said, "Naw, we don't mind. I would like to take Amy down to show her the cabin we built for her, though. I still haven't told her about it yet."

Daniel offered, "Well, after lunch, why don't you take her for a ride down there. Tell her you want to show her a place you've picked out to build a cabin. She'll be mighty surprised to see it already built."

Tommy said, "Yeah, that sounds like a good idea! Thanks, Daniel!"

The meal was cold, mostly fresh vegetables. Emily decided it was a special occasion, so she opened a jar of peaches and served them for dessert. Once they had finished, Daniel said, "Well, we'd better get back to that corn."

Amy asked, "Well, would you like some help? Tommy and me could come help you."

Daniel paused, then replied, "Well, that'd be great! Only, I think Tommy wants to show you something first. You two, take a little ride, then you can meet up with us later."

Tommy and Amy excused themselves, then walked out to the horses and mounted them. "Tommy? Where are we going?" Amy asked.

"Awe, I jest wonted ta show yuh where we could build our cabin someday."

Amy exclaimed, "Really! Oh, I'd love to see it."

Tommy replied, "Well, cum own then. Its jest on the other end of the valley. We can go down thar and have a look around, then we can change into some work clothes and come back."

They rode alongside the creek, moving toward the unknown cabin. They rode together, holding hands. Amy chattered constantly about what she wanted in a cabin. She was so excited about the prospect of building their own little house. She finally said, "Oh, Tommy! Can't you just see it?"

Tommy looked a little confused when he replied, "Well, naw. I can't see it yet."

Amy chuckled, "No, Tommy. I mean, can't you see it in your mind?"

Tommy said, "Oh, okay."

Amy questioned him then, "Wait, what did you mean?"

Tommy replied, "Nuttin'!"

As their ride swung to the right, the cabin finally came into view. When Amy caught sight of the cabin, she pulled her horse to a stop. "Tommy, who's cabin is that?"

Tommy lied when he said, "I don't rightly know. Let's check it out."

They rode slowly toward the cabin. Amy spied a longboard hanging from the front of the cabin with writing on it. When she got close enough to read it, her mouth dropped agape. The sign read, "*WELCOME HOME, TOMMY AND AMY.*" The letters had been burned into the wood with a branding iron.

"Tommy! You built me a cabin?"

Tommy replied, "Well, I had some help. Luke and James came and helped, and Daniel and Emily, of course."

Amy asked, "Can we go inside?"

"Well, shore! It's ours!"

Amy jumped from her horse and bound to the door when she heard, "Hold up there, now. Ain't I supposed to carry you over the threshold?"

Amy hopped up and down, waiting impatiently for Tommy to join her at the door. Tommy easily picked her up, then reached out with one hand to unlatch the door. The door swung open and exposed the inside to Amy. Amy gasped as she was carried in. "Oh, Tommy! It's precious! I love it!"

Tommy set her down so she could inspect everything. She marveled at the curtains that Emily had made for the window. Amy gasped at the little kitchen area that had already been supplied with pots, pans, and dishes. She ran her hand over the small square table in the middle of the room with two stools next to it. Then, she turned and saw the bed in the room's far corner. "Oh, Tommy! A real bed?"

Tommy saw it, too, for the first time. "Daniel and Emily must have made it after I left."

They both walked over to it to inspect it. It was built from logs, notched out, and fastened together. Ropes were knitted together to form the base where the mattress would lay. The mattress was homemade from an old quilt sewn together by hand and stuffed with feather ticking.

"Tommy! Can we try it out?"

Tommy replied, "Well, I don't see why not. We gotta be quick, though. Daniel is expecting us."

Amy said, "He won't mind. Besides, we gotta get undressed anyway. We might as well take advantage of the situation."

So, they did. They took advantage of the situation.

Chapter 15

At the end of the day, Daniel, Emily, Tommy, and Amy had completed all but fifteen acres of picking cutworms off the corn crop. They were all exhausted as they slowly made their way back to Daniel and Emily's cabin.

As they exited the cornfield, something caught Daniel's eye. A group of Indians rode slowly into the valley from the south. Daniel was a little concerned but not overly. These had been the first visitors to their valley since they had moved in, except for the Gordons. Daniel soon realized that there were two different tribes represented in the group. Four of the men were Chickasaw, although Daniel wasn't sure they were friendly. He wasn't sure what tribe the others represented.

As they approached, a tall Chickasaw man raised his right arm in a wave of greeting and said, "Hallito!".

"Hallito!" responded Daniel.

The man then said in English, "My name is Thomas Colbert. My father is Levi, brother of William Colbert."

Daniel replied, "Very nice to meet you, Thomas. I am Daniel Lane."

Thomas responded, "Yes. We know who you are. All of our people know who you are. They know your woman. We call her, Shobohli Eho. Woman who cures."

Daniel looked at Emily and introduced her to Thomas. "This is my wife, Emily. She is Shobohli Eho."

Emily bowed to Thomas in greeting. Daniel then asked, "Who are these other men?"

Thomas replied, "These three are my warriors. The other men are not Chickasaw. They are from the Wolf Clan of the Cherokee people. This one is Young Dragging Canoe. He is the son of Dragging Canoe. He needs help. He was attacked by a mountain lion two nights ago."

Daniel recognized the name Dragging Canoe. The father of this man was a chief of the Chickamauga tribe. They were a group of Cherokee who lived in north Georgia along the Chickamauga River. Dragging Canoe was at odds with most other Cherokee who lived in North Carolina and East Tennessee. Dragging Canoe's father, Attakullakulla, favored selling off part of their land to the white men in the late 1700s. Dragging Canoe opposed his father. In a prophetic speech *in 1775, Dragging Canoe proclaimed, "Whole Indian Nations have melted away like snowballs in the sun before the white man's advance."* He knew that the white man would continue to take land from the Cherokee. Just as they had the Delaware.

Daniel told Thomas, "Have your people set up camp over there by the creek. Emily will look to Young Dragging Canoe."

Two Cherokee men carried their chief and set him on a buffalo rug that one of the other men had spread out. Emily did a quick examination and found several deep cuts in his right thigh. The mountain lion's claws had made these deep gashes.

Emily asked Daniel, "Would you get my medical bag, please? Tommy, would you please get a fresh bucket of water?"

They did as she asked. Amy asked, "Is there anything I can do?"

Emily replied, "Why don't you get an oil lamp and light it. It's going to be dark soon." Amy did as Emily asked.

As Emily knelt on the ground next to the chief, she asked, "Do you speak English?"

Young Dragging Canoe replied, "I speak good English."

Emily said, "That's fine. I'm going to clean your wound and then sew it up so it will heal. I'll also give you something to swallow to keep the fever down. Alright?"

The chief responded, "Alright."

Daniel brought out the medical bag and handed it to Emily. He then stepped away and stood next to Thomas. Thomas asked Daniel, "What happened to your arm?"

Daniel said, "I was attacked by a bear about a month ago. It's almost healed up."

Thomas amusingly smiled and replied, "Hatuk app ala."

Daniel smiled when he realized Thomas had just given him a new name. Emily looked at them and asked, "What does it mean?"

Daniel replied, "He has given me a new name. Man Who Feeds Bears."

Emily responded, "I'm glad you think it's funny. You weren't laughing while I was sewing you up and setting your bones."

Daniel tried to hold back his smile as he glanced at Thomas.

Then Emily asked the chief, "When did this happen?"

Young Dragging Canoe answered, "Two days ago. On that ridge to the south above your valley."

Emily asked, "Why did you wait to seek help? You should have come down earlier."

The chief replied, "We don't trust white man. We could see you from the ridge. But totem say keep away."

Puzzled, Emily looked up at Thomas and asked, "Totem?"

Thomas said, "Chief William had his men place totems all around your valley. They warn all tribes to stay away. He wanted to make sure you stay safe. My men have been watching. We ride the hills keeping watch over you."

Emily wasn't sure whether she felt safer knowing that the Chickasaw were watching out for her safety or violated by not having any privacy.

While working on the chief's wounds, Emily asked, "Thomas, why do the Chickasaw take English names?"

"My grandfather was white. His name was James Colbert. He was born in North Carolina, but his mother and father were from Scotland. Grandfather traded with the Chickasaw. Then he married three times into the Chickasaw. Two women were full-blood Chickasaw. One was half-blood. My father is Levi, son of James and brother of William. I have a brother who is named David."

Daniel was excited by this. "I know David. He is a close friend. He taught me much when I first came into this land."

Thomas replied, "I spoke to David recently. He calls you, brother. Nafkl."

Jake growled a warning as he looked across Beaver Branch. Everyone turned to see what Jake was seeing. They watched as two men rode up to the branch with a mule in tow. They crossed the creek and rode into the camp. Daniel cautiously approached the men.

The older man looked to be about fifty. He was a man of the wilderness. Probably a trapper, Daniel thought. He had a short, scruffy beard, and his eyes were pale blue like the eyes of Daniel's sorrel horse. The other man was much younger. Barely a man. He was fidgety. He couldn't seem to sit still in his saddle. He never made eye contact with Daniel or anyone else.

"Good evenin', sir. Might you be Mr. Lane?" the old man asked.

"I'm Daniel Lane. May I ask your name?"

"My name is Samuel Tucker. Folks just call me Tuck. This here is my boy Seth. He don't talk a lot. Especially to strangers. But he's a good boy."

Daniel asked, "What can I do for you, Tuck?"

"Well, sir. We just came from the Gordon place. We was doing some tradin'. I'm a trapper. So we sold off some furs we had stored up. I've been havin' an awful toothache for a couple weeks now. Mrs. Gordon said ya'll have a doctor of sorts over here. Said I should get the doc to take a look at my tooth. I got some money, so I'm willin' to pay for your services."

Daniel said, "Well, Tuck, I'm not the doctor. My wife does the doctoring around here."

Daniel presented Emily with a wave of his hand. Emily, still sewing up the chief's wounds, nodded toward Tuck.

Emily said, "Daniel, set them up over by the river, and I'll take a look when I'm finished here."

Daniel took Tuck and Seth down to the Duck and helped them find a suitable spot to set up camp for the night. A half-hour later, Emily showed up carrying her medical bag and a lamp. Emily looked over at Seth as she entered their campsite. She noticed how he kept fidgeting, rocking back and forth as he sat beside the fire. "Don't mind him none, ma'am. He's harmless."

Emily asked, "Does he speak?"

"Yessum, but not much. Sometimes, its just a bunch of jibber jab. Nothin' I can understand. But now, he's real good with numbers!. He ain't stupid like most folk thinks. He's just, differn't."

Emily asked, "Does he have something that he delights in? Say, a hobby? Something that holds his attention?"

Tuck replied, "Birds. He loves birds. And he collects feathers, although now, he don't pull them off the birds. He just finds them layin' on the ground or on a tree branch sometimes. He would never hurt them."

"Sounds like your son is autistic," Emily diagnosed.

"Ah, no ma'am. He ain't much with drawin' or paintin' nor nuthin'.

" Emily replied, "No, Mr. Tucker. You misunderstood me. Autistic, not artistic. Autism is a condition in the brain. It's hard to describe or even to understand. He's not sick or crazy or even slow. He's just different, as you said. His brain works completely differently from yours or mine. He's special!"

Tuck looked at Emily with understanding and respect and replied, "Yes, ma'am! He is special!"

"Alright, Mr. Tucker.", she said. "Let's have a look at that mouth. Open up!"

She handed Daniel the lamp and then moved his arm around until she had the light positioned just right to see into the old man's mouth. She took a tongue depressor from her bag and moved it around in his mouth, searching for the problem. "Have you been drinking, Mr. Tucker?"

Tuck replied, "Well, just swishin' it around in my mouth a bit to help with the pain, ma'am."

Emily then asked, "You chew tobacco, don't you?"

"Yessum," he replied.

"Well, you need to stop.", Emily announced. "Not only is it a nasty habit, it will kill you. You've got some leukoplakia developing in there. But that's not your problem right now. You also have an abscessed tooth. I can't do anything about that tonight. We'll take care of it in the morning."

She reached into her bag and found a small bottle of clove oil. She opened the bottle and then dipped a cotton swab into it. She swabbed the inside of his mouth with the swab. The smell of the cloves was overpowering, but the clove oil numbed Tuck's mouth immediately. "See if that won't hold you till morning. Then, we'll see about removing that tooth.

Meanwhile, no more tobacco. That leukoplakia will turn into cancer if you're not careful. If you quit using tobacco, you should be alright. For a while, at least."

The next morning, Emily got started early, preparing breakfast for all the guests scattered around their home. Amy and Tommy showed up early to help. They had already eaten. Emily made three Dutch ovens of biscuits to serve to the guests. She served them with honey and bacon, which she fried.

Emily turned to Tuck after breakfast and asked, "Well, Mr. Tucker, are you ready to get rid of that rotten tooth?"

"Yes, ma'am!" he replied. "Only one thing. How much do you need for your services?"

Emily answered, "Well, we can worry about that afterward."

Tuck said, "If it's all the same to you, ma'am, I'd like to settle up first. I might not be in such a generous mood afterward if you know what I mean."

Emily replied, "Well, alright, how does a dollar sound to you?"

Tuck said, "That'll be jest fine, ma'am." Tuck reached into a poke he carried at his waist, pulled out a silver coin, and handed it to Emily.

Emily said to Amy, "Would you do me a favor? I think Seth would like to see our chickens. Would you mind taking him back there and showing them to him? Show him how we collect the eggs."

Amy nodded in understanding that Emily didn't want Seth to see what she was about to do to his father. Emily continued, "It should take you about thirty minutes."

Amy said, "Okay. Seth, would you like to see our chickens?"

Seth grunted a reply and said, "Chickens! Bok! Bok! Bok!" Then he followed Amy to the coop.

When they returned to the coop, the chickens were already scattered about, searching for food on the ground. Seth glanced at the fowl scattered across the small field and said, "Twenty-nine chickens!"

Amazed at his ability to count them so quickly, Amy replied, "That's right, Seth! Would you like to feed them?"

She took a bucket of corn out of the barn, gave it to Seth, and said, "Just a little at a time, now. Like this."

She reached into the bucket, scooped up some corn with her small hand, and tossed it toward the chickens. "Chick, chick, chick, chick!"

Amy called them. Seth was delighted to see the birds come toward her and scramble after the fallen kernels of corn. He imitated her song and tossed the corn to the chickens, laughing as he did. "Chick, chick. Chick, chick."

While Amy kept Seth busy and away from the others, Emily instructed the men to bring a table outside from inside the cabin. They set it up in front of the cabin, where there would be plenty of daylight. She had Tuck lie on the table, on his back. Emily rolled up a bath towel and placed it behind his neck to help support his head and keep it tilted backward so she could better see into his mouth. Emily deadened his mouth as best she could with the clove oil. Then she took a pair of forceps from her bag and went to work on the tooth. Tuck immediately began to squirm. "Daniel, Tommy, I need you to hold him down."

They each obliged, each man taking a side and holding him down as best they could.

Emily rocked the forceps back and forth as she gripped the tooth with them. Tuck began moaning with discomfort. Emily said, "Tuck, try not to yell. We don't want to upset Seth."

The Chickasaw and Chickamauga men became curious and moved in for a closer look. They encircled the table to watch. Tuck's legs began to flail with each tug of the forceps. "Hold his legs down!" Emily demanded.

Four of the men braced themselves against Tuck's legs, pinning him to the table.

Tuck's moans were growing into wails. "Hang in there, Tuck.", Emily encouraged him. "We're almost done."

Emily could feel the tooth loosening, but the forceps were losing their grip. She relaxed temporarily, then repositioned the forceps to get a better hold on the rotten tooth. Then, with one hard tug, the tooth came free. "Got it!" Emily triumphantly announced.

She set the forceps, holding the extracted tooth, aside. Then, she began packing Tuck's jaw with cotton gauze. "Okay, Tuck. Try to relax for a minute. Let's see if we can stop the bleeding a bit."

Emily kept checking and replacing the gauze. Finally, the bleeding slowed, so she rolled up a small amount of the dressing and placed it in the empty area of Tuck's mouth that the tooth had once occupied.

Tuck and Emily were both drenched in sweat. Emily used the back of her hand to wipe away the sweat from her brow. "Daniel. Get this man a drink of whiskey. He's earned it."

Daniel did as Emily instructed, and Tuck readily accepted the drink. Tuck sat up on the edge of the table to enjoy his drink. Suddenly, Seth and Amy came striding around the corner of the cabin. Seth was delightedly carrying one of the hens while petting her. "Chicken! Bok bok", he said.

Everyone smiled and giggled at Seth's delight and at his ignorance of the ordeal his father had just been through.

CHAPTER 16

Samuel and Seth said "*good-bye*" to everyone and made their way back across the Beaver, heading northeast. Seth smiled all along the way as he caressed a tiny fluffy creature that rested in the palm of his hand. Emily had given Seth a baby chick to carry with him on his journey. He and his father would return north toward Kentucky to trap more furs.

Tommy and Daniel moved back into the cornfield to finish picking cutworms off the corn in the final fifteen acres. Amy and Emily stayed close to the cabin, caring for the livestock and tending to the garden. Emily wanted to be close by should Young Dragging Canoe need her. Thomas and one of his braves followed Daniel into the cornfield to observe what they were doing more closely.

After Emily and Amy had finished feeding the livestock, Emily decided to take the mules out of the corral and give them some exercise. She and Amy took lead reins into the corral and snapped them to the mules' halters. Amy led Rusty, and Emily led Pepper out of the corral and closed the gate behind them. Amy and Emily led the mules to the front of the cabin. When the Cherokee men saw the giants walking toward them, they stood in awe. They murmured in their native tongues to one another at how massive the animals were. The two giants towered over the men and their ponies. The ponies, tied to a picket line, scrambled around, attempting to break free. They whinnied with fright at the massive unknown beasts that hovered over them.

Young Dragging Canoe cautiously approached Emily and asked, "What is it?"

Emily replied, "These are my two mules. This is Pepper, and that one is Rusty."

The young chief then asked, "I have never seen such animals as these. Where do they come from?"

Emily explained, "Well back in England and other places in Europe, there are large horses. They call them draft horses. They are used to pull heavy loads. You know what a donkey is, right?"

He responded, "Yes, I have seen donkeys. They are very small, though."

Emily replied, "Yes, that's right. But when you breed a donkey to a horse, you get a mule. And if you breed a donkey to a draft horse, you get a huge mule. Pepper and Rusty had Belgian mothers and donkey fathers."

Young Dragging Canoe was amazed at the animals. He and his men surrounded the mules and touched them as if they were unsure if they were *actually* seeing them.

The young chief then asked Emily, "How strong are they?"

Emily thought momentarily, then replied, "One of my mules is probably as strong as four of your ponies."

Young Dragging Canoe's eyes widened in response. He said, "These are good strong ponies. They are stronger than they look."

Emily got a sly little gleam in her eyes, then asked, "You want to try it?"

The young chief replied with a smile, "I do. But, we must make a wager. If I win, I get your mule. If you win, you get one of my ponies."

Emily scoffed. "The bet is one mule against four ponies. If I win, I get four ponies, not one."

Young Dragging Canoe sighed and thought momentarily before replying, "Let it be done!"

Emily led Pepper back to the corral and cinched the lead rein to one of the fence's rails. She went into the shelter, retrieved a harness, and draped it over Pepper's back. Once she got the harness buckled in place and tightened, she led Pepper back out to meet his opponents. Emily asked two men to roll an eight-foot log into the area where the pull would occur. She hitched up Pepper's harness to the log, then waited for the opponents to do likewise.

The Indians brought four of their ponies over to the log and used ropes to connect the ponies to the log on the opposite side from Pepper. Emily drove a stake into the ground that lined up with Pepper's nose. She then did the same at the other end, driving a stake in the dirt to line up with the ponies' noses. "Your ponies need to pull my mule past this stake to win. My mule wins if he pulls your ponies past that other stake. Agreed?"

The chief said, "Agreed!"

Emily was confident, not only in Pepper's strength but in his pulling ability and his experience. He was bred for this sort of competition. The ponies were used to men on their backs, but she was sure they had rarely been used to pull anything. Emily positioned herself behind Pepper and just to the right. She used the long reins she typically used while driving the wagon to guide him. The Indians chose to pull their animals from the front. That alone would put them at a disadvantage because the ponies would naturally pull against someone trying to lead them in this way.

Emily looked over at the chief who was standing to the side of the setup. She nodded to him and said, "You make the call."

Young Dragging Canoe checked his men and then Emily. When he was satisfied that everyone was ready, he raised his fist in the air and let out a "whoop" to begin the competition.

All at once, his men started yelling at their ponies, coaxing them to move forward. Emily steadily encouraged Pepper by saying, "Steady, Pepper!"

Pepper felt the tug of the ponies behind him but stood his ground. He lowered his haunches, digging his hind legs into the ground to hold the ponies at bay. Emily encouraged her mighty giant to stand firm. Pepper stood firm. He had barely moved from his spot. The ponies were rising on their hindquarters while they didn't comprehend what was expected of them. Being somewhat annoyed, Pepper looked around to see what was behind him. When he realized the ponies were pulling against him, he decided it was time to go to work. He bore down, gaining traction in his hind feet, then lunged forward, moving one steady step at a time.

When Emily saw that Pepper was ready, she let out an ear-piercing whistle and yelled out, "Yaw, Pepper!"

Pepper moved forward steadily but slowly.

Nearly a quarter of a mile away, Daniel and Tommy, along with the two Indians, were still picking cutworms off of the corn stalks when Daniel heard Emily's whistle. Daniel froze in his tracks and held up a hand to stop Tommy. They all heard yelling and screaming in the distance. Daniel's heart sank at the thought that Emily and Amy were under attack. Daniel suddenly dropped his bucket and yelled, "Let's go!"

He ran back toward the cabin, Tommy and the Indians following behind. Minutes later, they bound out of the cornfield into the open field on which the cabin lay. There, he balked, gasping for air. He bent over with his uninjured arm resting on his knee as he watched, then slowly walked down to where everyone was gathered.

"Yaw, Pepper!" Emily encouraged him. Pepper started gaining ground with surprisingly little effort. The ponies realized something was pulling them back, and they began to panic even more. They whinnied and moaned as they struggled against the pull from this giant they had encountered. The Indians leading them were pulling with all their might, not realizing they were making it even more difficult for the ponies. The ponies didn't know whether to pull against their leaders or the giant.

Emily spoke in a steady voice, encouraging Pepper, "Good boy, Pepper. Up! Up!"

Pepper grunted and let out a snort. He lunged forward again and pulled the ponies and their leaders back toward his stake—just six feet more to win. Emily spoke again, "Come on, boy! Move up! Up! Up!"

Pepper surged forward again; this time, it was enough to end the competition. Emily raised her hands in victory, letting loose of the reins. She heard cheering from the men as they made their way toward her from the cornfield. She walked up to Pepper, stroked his face and the side of his head, and then said, "That's my good boy. What a good boy."

Daniel ran to Emily and grabbed her, lifting her up to him with his good arm. "I don't know what this is all about but, congratulations!"

When he set her back down, she said, "I'll tell you later."

She then moved toward Young Dragging Canoe and held out her hand to him. "What do you think? Are you satisfied?"

The chief smirked an annoying little smile and responded, "They are now your ponies."

Emily smiled and said, "Thanks, but you're going to need those ponies to get where you're going. I trust you. Next time you come through, you can bring me my ponies."

The chief smiled and said, "Agreed!"

That night, after supper, Daniel found time to sit and read more from Gus's diary.

September 10, 1774

We saw a large band of Indians traveling through the Salt Lick area today. We kept our distance. I asked if Timothy knew who they were. He said they were Cherokee. He pointed out a chief to me who was near the front of the caravan. He said that he was Dragging Canoe. He told me this chief led a band of Cherokee that lived along the Chickamauga River in the south. He was the meanest and smartest of all Cherokee. He was a fierce-looking man, even from a distance. He was tall, about six feet, and was built like an Oak tree. I hope that I never meet this man face to face.

How odd that he happened upon this passage in Gus's diary after having just met the son of this great Cherokee warrior. Daniel wished he had known more about Gus's life on this side of the Shimmering while they had spent time together. Gus had been more interested in things of the 21st Century than sharing his experiences with Daniel.

October 30, 1774

Timothy says we will continue to trap throughout the winter. Then, he plans to travel back to Illinois in the spring to sell the furs. I will go with him this time. He said I should not only know how to trap and prepare the pelts, but I should also know about trading and selling them as well.

I look forward to traveling with him on the river.

Chapter 17

June 10, 1819

When the Lanes woke up, it was a muggy summer morning. Their visitors had left two days earlier. Tommy and Daniel had met at first light to go hunting. They took their rifles and walked south along the forest's edge to begin their hunt.

Emily and Amy each took care of their baking for the week. Emily made four large loaves of bread and then decided a cake would be lovely. The milking and egg gathering would come first, however. While the bread baked in the stove, they would churn butter too.

The men returned within an hour of leaving for their hunt. Tommy carried a buck deer over his shoulders while Daniel carried his and Tommy's rifles. They had field-dressed the deer in the woods. They chose not to skin the deer or butcher it until later. They had other chores to deal with first. They cared for the livestock and then checked on the corn again to make sure it was still doing well.

After lunch, Daniel spent some time chopping firewood to keep their store filled. He still wore the sling, so he had to split the wood one-handed. Jake was lying in the front yard, chewing on a piece of deer bone he had scavenged. In the distance, across the Beaver, Jake heard some rustling. He let out a *"woof."*

Daniel looked up from his ax swinging and searched for whatever might have gotten Jake's attention. Jake stood and began barking as he saw a large group of riders coming down the trail toward the creek bank. Daniel raised his hand to shade his eyes from the sun as he wondered who might be visiting them this time. Emily came out of the house to check on the commotion, wiping her hands on her apron.

Daniel counted twenty-eight riders crossing Beaver Creek and riding into their farm. Many of the faces were familiar to him. Especially the rider in the lead. Daniel sank his ax blade into the stump he used to split the firewood, then greeted the men.

"Mr. Lane, it's good to see you again."

Daniel reached up to shake the man's hand and replied, "Well, Colonel Crockett. What brings you here?"

"We're on our way back to Lawrenceburg from Nashville. When we got to the Gordon's place, I asked Mrs. Gordon if she had heard from you lately. She informed me that you were homesteading here in this valley. We thought we'd come by and say, howdy."

"Well, howdy!" said Daniel. "Get down and make yourselves at home."

Then Daniel turned slightly toward Emily and said to Crockett, "Colonel, I'd like you to meet my wife, Emily."

Crockett stepped down from his horse and shook hands with Emily. "Ma'am, it is very nice to meet you. How are all of you settling in here?"

Emily replied, "We're doing well. We love it here in our little valley."

Daniel turned toward Tommy and said, "Colonel, I'd like you to meet my partner, Tommy Brown."

Crockett shook hands with Tommy and said, "Very nice to make your acquaintance, Mr. Brown."

Tommy replied, "Uh, call me Tommy. It's very nice to meet you too."

A squeal came from the cornfield, and everyone turned to see Amy galloping toward them. She screamed and called out as she ran toward them, "Davy! Davy Crockett! What are you doing here?"

She sprinted to Crockett and jumped into his arms to hug him. "Well, howdy, Amy! What are you doing here?"

As he let her down to the ground, she replied, "I live here now. I got married to Tommy. I'm now Mrs. Amy Brown."

Emily commented, "Well, I see you two know each other."

Crockett replied, "I've known Amy since she was just a sprout. Me and her go way back."

Emily said, "Well, we just finished lunch, but I'm sure we can scrounge something up for you and your men."

"Don't bother," said Crockett. "We ate in the saddle on our way here. We would like to set up camp for the night if you don't mind."

Emily replied, "We wouldn't have it any other way."

Daniel said, "Why don't we finish skinning that deer Tommy killed this morning and get it started cooking for our evening meal? It should be plenty for everyone."

Emily said, "That sounds fine. We'll make a party of it. Amy and I can do some more baking to make sure there's enough bread and cake for everyone."

Once Crockett's men dismounted and began setting up camp, an older man wandered over to Daniel. "How's your head, young feller?"

It was Doc Simmons. Simmons had nursed Daniel back from injury after being clubbed by Prissy Griner at Grinder's stand. Daniel saw him and exclaimed, "Well, hello, Doc! How are you?"

Simmons replied, "Oh, fair to middlin'. I see yore stove up again, though."

Daniel replied, "Yeah, I had a run-in with a bear a few weeks back. It's about all healed up, though. Emily says I can take the sling off next week."

"Emily?" asked Simmons.

Daniel replied, "Doc, this is my wife, Emily. She's also our resident medicine woman."

"Well, please to meet you, Ma'am! I've never met a genuine medicine woman before."

Emily replied, "Well, that's what Daniel calls me. I was actually trained as a nurse."

Simmons then said, "Educated, huh? Maybe you could teach me a few things then."

Emily replied, "I doubt it, but if I can, I'd be happy to."

Daniel and Tommy were about to set up a spit to start a fire when Crockett suggested, "Why don't you let my cook take care of all that so we can visit?"

Daniel said, "That sounds great!"

Crockett called out for a man named Akers, who promptly ran forward to be instructed. "Akers, you and your cooks get that deer skint and started cooking."

Akers replied, "Sure thing, Davy ... uh Colonel."

Everyone pitched in, getting everything ready for the evening meal. Emily and Amy finished the baking while Colonel Crockett's men cooked everything else. They set up makeshift buffet tables out of boards lying across sawhorses. As the men finished the cooking, Emily and Amy joined Tommy, Daniel, and Davy on the front porch to visit. Amy asked Davy about Nashville to catch up on the local gossip. Jake came over and nestled between Daniel's legs, nudging him with his nose and coaxing him to pet Jake's head.

The day was a waste as far as getting any work done around the farm. It was a success, however, in creating new friendships and nurturing old ones. Emily was ecstatic inside that she met her relative, who was considered the patriarch of Lawrence County. She wished she could talk to her grandpa now and tell him she *actually* got to meet the world-famous David Crockett.

Later in the evening, everyone gathered around the buffet tables to begin partaking in the feast. The venison and all of the side dishes prepared by the militia cooks were delicious. Emily and Amy's fresh bread and cakes were particularly big hits with the men. They were rare treats to men who mostly survived on hardtack and jerky.

At some point in the evening, someone brought out a fiddle and began to play. Several of the men joined in to sing some old familiar songs. Once in a while, the fiddler would play a lively tune to which some of the men enjoyed dancing.

Later in the evening, Emily found an opportunity to meet with Crockett face to face as things began to die down a little. They sat together on the front porch alone. Emily stepped inside the cabin momentarily, then came back out, holding a small ornate chest. "Colonel Crockett, I was wondering if I could impose upon you for a favor?"

Crockett looked at Emily, then looked at the chest she held in her lap. "What is it you want from me?"

Emily took out a small key and unlocked the little chest. "Inside this chest is a letter." She pulled out the envelope and showed it to him. "I need someone in your family to please deliver this letter for me."

Crockett replied, "I don't see that as a problem. As long as they don't live halfway across the world somewhere."

Emily continued, "They don't. But, the thing is, it can't be delivered for about two-hundred years."

This took Crockett by surprise. "How am I supposed to deliver a letter for you two-hundred years from now?"

Emily replied, "Not you. Someone in your family two-hundred years from now. Think of it as a time capsule. Can you imagine receiving a box from someone that was sealed back in the sixteen hundreds? Just think of the delight in finding something like that."

Davy replied, "Well, I guess that would be very intriguing. But how will they know when to open it? And how will they know it's for them?"

Emily told him, "Look at the name on the envelope."

He read, "Emily Lane." He thought for a while before speaking again. "I'm not sure I understand still. Isn't that your name?"

Emily replied, "I'm not sure that I can explain that to you, so you will believe me. Let's just say I'm hoping that someone by that name will show up in your family lineage at just the right time."

"Just when is the right time?"

Emily answered, "December 22, 2017. All you need to do is keep it safe, and keep it a secret. Only you can know about this until you feel your life is coming to an end. Then, pass it down to one of your sons with the same instructions I have given you. Ask him to do the same. Can you do that for me?"

Davy said, "It's very curious, this thing you ask of me. As long as I can keep it a secret, I guess I can handle it. I wouldn't want folks to be thinking I was addle. So I'll do as you ask."

Emily said, "Thank you so much. I know you can't imagine why, but this is very important to me."

Davy took Emily's chest and placed it in his tent. Then they both returned to the party. Crockett eventually made his way to Daniel and asked, "Mr. Lane, don't be offended by my words, but is your wife reliable?"

Daniel looked at him curiously and said, "Ah! She gave you the chest, didn't she?"

Crockett nodded. "Emily Crockett Lane is the smartest, most compassionate, most loyal person I have ever known."

Davy was stunned by Daniel's statement, stared in amazement, and then asked, "Did you say, Emily Crockett Lane?"

"She didn't tell you? You and Emily are very distant kin. She was a Crockett before she married me."

Chapter 18

Daniel woke early the next morning before daylight. He had been dreaming of Gus. Daniel couldn't remember much about the dream, but it stirred him. He began to worry that Gus didn't return home after all. Daniel couldn't help but feel his friend was in danger. He told himself that it was silly to feel that way. It was merely a dream and didn't mean anything. Gus was fine. He was probably back home with his mom and dad, catching up on all that had happened to him over the past forty-six years.

He decided that it was useless. He was wide awake and not likely to fall back to sleep. He very carefully extracted himself from the bed, trying not to wake Emily. He quietly dressed, grabbed an oil lamp and Gus's diary, and went outside to read.

He was surprised to see some of the militia moving around. The cooks were already preparing breakfast for the company. Daniel nodded to one of the men as he sat down on the porch. He lit the oil lamp and opened the diary to read.

September 7, 1775
I haven't been feeling well. I think I have a cold. I hope it isn't the flu. I've been hanging around camp for the last two days, getting as much rest as I can.

Today, I saw Red Coats traveling through the forest. I counted around fifty of them. I could see them

moving down next to the Cumberland River. Near dusk, they had marched out of sight, but I could see smoke rising through the trees to the north. I'm sure they had made camp for the night. I hope it is for only one night. I don't want anything to do with them.

When Timothy got back to camp, he said he had not seen them. I think it is a good thing that he didn't. I'm not too sure how friendly they would be to a Frenchman.

October 4, 1775

Timothy says we should pack up and go back north for the winter. We've got a vast store of pelts to carry with us. I don't look forward to going north for the winter, but Timothy has a cabin to keep us warm instead of staying in a cave all winter. We'll leave in two days.

October 8, 1775

While floating along the Tennessee River today, we happened upon a small band of Indians. Timothy said they were

Shawnee. He spoke to them in French, and one of them

understood. Timothy said he asked them about his missing wife. They claimed to not know anything about her. They wanted us to give them all of our furs. They said it was

payment for using their river. Timothy refused and told them it wasn't their river; it was his, and they should give us all of their furs. Timothy and I both raised our rifles at them to show we weren't going to back down. They only had bows and arrows, so

they backed off and continued downriver. Timothy is a brave man, but someday, I think he might get us killed.

Gus and Timothy had been on the water for three days. They had made the exchange from the Cumberland River to the Tennessee River two days ago. They were now traveling up the Ohio River, where the water was reasonably calm. The rain had been scarce recently. Timothy's boat was loaded heavily because they had a good year of trapping. Fox, beaver, muskrat, rabbit, bear, and deer hides were tanned and ready for market. The hull of the small boat was full. Timothy draped canvas over the tops of the pelts to keep them as dry as possible. Timothy was happy to have Gus along on this trip because the boat was much easier to control with two men rather than trying to control it by himself.

They traveled northwest along the river. If all went well, Timothy and Gus would reach the Kaskaskia River tomorrow. As they rounded the bend, Gus spotted three canoes in the distance. "Timothy!" he yelled back.

Timothy looked ahead from his place at the back of the boat. When he saw the vessels coming toward them, he said to Gus, "Get ready! We may be in for a fight."

Gus reached for his rifle and unwrapped it from the oilcloth he used to cover the firing mechanism. The cloth was meant to keep the gun's powder dry from water that would periodically splash into the boat. Gus checked to see if his powder was still dry. It was. He kept the rifle at his side. He wanted to be ready but didn't want to seem confrontational.

Timothy yelled out a greeting in French, "Bonjour!"

One of the Indians returned the greeting. Six men were traveling together. They, too, had a few furs in their canoes, but not nearly as many as Gus and Timothy. Timothy and the Indian continued their conversation in French. The man he spoke to was tall and wiry. Whenever he and Timothy spoke to one another, Timothy would try to keep Gus informed by translating their phrases into English under his breath to Gus.

Timothy said to Gus, "They are Shawnee. I have asked them if they know of my wife. He claims to not have heard of any white women being held captive by his people. I think he is a liar."

Then, the braves picked up their bows and pointed arrows toward Timothy and Gus. Another phrase was spoken. Timothy translated, "He says that we are traveling on their river, and we must pay. He wants all of our furs."

"What?" said Gus.

Timothy said to Gus, "Point your rifle at them."

Gus did as he was told. His stomach churned, and his heart began to pound in his chest. Even though a cool breeze was blowing across the open water, Gus began to sweat. Then, Timothy spoke to the Shawnee again.

He translated to Gus, "I have told them it is not their river, it is ours They must give us all of their furs."

Gus heard Timothy cock his rifle from behind his head. Gus did the same. The two of them pointed their guns directly at the Shawnee man who spoke. The man was a little concerned but said to Timothy, "You cannot kill us all. We will overcome you before you can reload."

Timothy replied, "We don't have to kill all of you. But, you will be the first to be killed."

The man considered this for a moment. When he saw that both rifles were pointed directly at him, he knew it was true. He would likely not make it out alive if he persisted. He chose to back down. He said something to his men, who all lay down their bows. He then said to Timothy, "You may continue."

Timothy told Gus, "Keep your gun pointed at him while I get us clear of here."

Gus continued to point his gun at the man until their boat was out of range of the canoes.

April 2, 1778

I can't believe it! I just met Daniel Boone! Timothy and I were coming back to Tennessee from Illinois. We stopped for the night and camped along the Ohio River through Kentucky. Some men came to our camp and asked to share our fire. One of them was very tall. He turned out to be Daniel Boone. They were out on a journey to find salt for their community. He didn't look anything like Fess Parker from the TV show.

Daniel snickered to himself about Gus's reference to Fess Parker just as Colonel Crockett walked up.

"Whatcha readin'?" he asked.

Daniel replied, "Oh, it's a diary written by a friend of mine. Do you remember Gus Childers? He used to run Gordon's Ferry."

Davy replied, "Yeah, older feller? White beard? Real talkative."

Daniel replied, "Yeah, that's old Gus."

Crockett then asked, "What happened to him?"

Daniel answered, "He went back home. Somewhere between Columbia and Lawrenceburg, I think."

"Well, maybe we'll run into him on the way back home," said Crockett. "You know where his home is?"

"No, I don't. Gus said it was called the Grove, but I don't know where it is. He left this diary for me as a gift. It holds about forty-five years of history in it. Gus knew how much I love to study history."

Davy asked, "Speaking of diaries and such, whatever became of that journal you had? The one Meriweather Lewis was supposed to have written."

Daniel replied, "I've still got it. It's inside. If you want it, I'll get it for you after Emily wakes. I want her to sleep as much as possible. She's expecting, you know."

"No, I didn't know. Well, congratulations! When do you expect her to deliver?

"Probably late December. Who knows, we might have ourselves a Christmas baby."

Davy said, "Wouldn't that be something? Back to the journal, don't you want to keep it? It being history and all."

Daniel said, "No, I don't think so. It's kind of like you told me before. History and the truth seldom coincide. It's not going to do me any good. Maybe you can use it in some way. You can have the ledgers too."

The colonel said, "Well, I'll let you get back to your reading. I'm gonna check on the men."

Chapter 19

June 11, 1819

Daniel awoke suddenly from a deep sleep because a clatter from outside had stirred him. Emily was already up and preparing breakfast. Daniel dragged himself out of bed and dressed. He opened the cabin door to see what the commotion was outside. Crockett's men were packing up their gear and preparing to leave.

Daniel walked among the men as they were busy breaking down their camp. He shook hands and said goodbye to many of them with whom he had become friendly. Daniel found Doc Simmons and talked with him before turning away in search of the Colonel. There, he stood in solitude at the edge of the Duck River. Daniel walked over to join him.

"Colonel? Sorry, I don't mean to disturb you. I just wanted to say goodbye since you and your men seem to be packing up to leave."

"Don't you think it's about time you started calling me David or even Davy? After all, we're evidently related."

Daniel responded, "Sure. Well, I know you must have a million questions about Emily and me. I just wish I knew how to explain it all."

"Yeah, I've got a powerful lot of questions. I don't understand why your wife would ask me to deliver a letter she wrote to herself. Or why it can't be delivered until two-hundred years from now. But I do know this, you two are good, fine people. You're just trying to carve out a living for yourselves here in this valley. And, I'm glad I've gotten to know you."

Daniel replied, "Thanks, but I'd like to try to explain if I can. Have you ever heard of Ittola Chuka?"

Davy thought momentarily, then replied, "Some sort of Chickasaw taboo, isn't it?"

Daniel said, "It's more than that. The words translate, shimmering door. Ittola Chuka is a time portal. It led me, and Emily here from our world two-hundred years from now."

Crockett asked, "Are they all that way?"

Daniel asked, "Are what all that way?"

"Ittola Chuka. Are all of them time portals?"

Daniel couldn't believe what he was hearing. "There are more than one?"

Davy replied, "Yep. I know of at least five places the Chickasaw call Ittola Chuka. They keep a close watch on all of them too."

"Davy, is there any chance you could sketch out a quick map of the locations you know about?"

Davy replied, "Sure, but why don't you ask your friend David Colbert. He knows where all of them are."

Stunned, Daniel slowly said, "I think I'll just do that." Then he said, "You will come by and say goodbye to Emily before you leave?"

"I will. I'll be there directly."

Daniel then said, "Thanks, Davy. Thanks for everything."

Within the hour, the men had packed up the camp and were ready to ride. Davy rode up to the cabin just as Emily was walking outside. He stepped down from his horse and approached Emily with his hand extended.

"Emily, it was a pleasure meeting you. I hope to see you again someday."

"Thank you, David. I look forward to it. And, thanks for taking care of that chest for me."

"It's my pleasure. Goodbye."

Crockett mounted his horse and commanded the men to move out. They crossed over the ridge on the south side of the valley as they rode toward Lawrenceburg. Emily wondered if she would ever see him again.

Just before noon, a carriage appeared on the rise above the valley. It moved along the trail coming from the north. There were two riders following the wagon. The horsemen were well-armed, and they were wearing black frock coats. The driver of the carriage was well-dressed and well-groomed. There were two passengers. There was a young woman who appeared to be only about sixteen and a gentleman at least fifteen years older.

Emily greeted them as they drove up to the cabin. "Good morning! Are you folks lost?" she asked.

The carriage driver asked, "Are you, Mrs. Lane?"

"I am. How may I help you?"

"We were told by Mrs. Gordon that a doctor lives here. Is the doctor here?"

Emily explained, "I guess you are looking for me. I'm the only one here who practices medicine. Is someone sick?"

The driver said, "Mrs. Van Dusan needs some attention if you please."

Emily replied, "Why of coarse. Please step down."

The man and woman in the back of the carriage stepped out and walked toward Emily. They were dressed in expensive clothing, and Emily could tell they were well-to-do. The young woman gingerly walked as they approached Emily.

"Mrs. Lane, I am Charles Van Dusan, and this is my wife, Susan. We are traveling to New Orleans from Richmond. My wife is suffering from an ailment of a delicate nature. Might you be able to help her?"

Emily replied, "I certainly will try. Mrs. Van Dusan, won't you come in?"

They both moved onto the cabin's porch when Emily turned to the gentleman and said, "Mr. Van Dusan, it might be best if you wait out here."

"I don't see why!" he exclaimed.

Emily said, "Let's just say it can get a little crowded in there, and I need plenty of room to work. Besides, in times like these, your wife deserves a little discretion. Don't you agree?"

Without saying another word, Van Dusan allowed the women to proceed without him. Emily opened the door to the cabin to let her patient in. Jake was lying under the table. "Jake, outside boy!"

Jake lazily got up and walked outside to find a new spot to sleep. Emily asked, "Alright, what seems to be the problem?"

The young woman began to speak, "Well, I've got this terrible rash developing between my legs. You know, in the nether region?"

Susan Van Dusan spoke with a long southern drawl. She was stunning and very proper. She reminded Emily of some genteel ladies in ***Gone with the Wind***.

Susan came from a very well-to-do family in Virginia. Her father, Richard Claiborne, owned one of the most extensive plantations in Virginia. He was also an exporter, exporting sugar, tobacco, and cotton into Europe by way of his own fleet of ships.

Susan was very sheltered while growing up in Virginia. She was well-educated yet ignorant of the ways of the world. Susan was well-read and dreamed of seeing the world outside the plantation, where she had lived her whole life. The only contact she had ever made with men was when her family would throw parties in their extravagant ballroom. The young men who attended these balls were rich, pampered, egotistical, and annoying to Susan. So when Charles Van Dusan walked into her life, she found him exciting, experienced and well-traveled. Or, at least, that is what he led her to believe.

Emily asked, "When did it start?"

Susan replied, "A couple of days ago. We were already out of Nashville when I started itching something awful. The more I scratched, the more I itched."

Emily asked, "Do you mind if I take a look? It might just be a yeast infection. But, we should make sure it isn't something more serious."

"Alright," Susan replied.

Emily suggested, "Why don't you strip down to your undergarments. Take your bloomers off too. I'll give you a sheet you can cover with."

Susan did as Emily instructed. Emily took a blanket and stretched it over the table. Then, she had Susan lie on the table for the examination.

"How long have you been married?"

"Just three weeks."

Emily looked under the sheet covering the young woman and found what she had expected. It appeared to be nothing more than a yeast infection. Emily mixed up some oils for Susan. She poured some oregano oil with lavender and coconut oil into a small vial. Emily applied some of the mixture to the infected area, then said, "Alright, you can get dressed. It's just a yeast infection. I think we can take care of that pretty easily."

She handed the vial to Susan and instructed, "Rub a few drops on the infected area before you get dressed in the morning and at night before you go to bed. If the itching persists, just excuse yourself to the privy and apply another dose. Avoid sitting in soapy water for too long. Just get in, wash up, and get out. The most important thing is after you and your husband have had sexual intercourse, excuse yourself and go to the privy again. Urinating will flush out any bacteria that might cause an infection. Okay?"

After the young lady dressed, Emily escorted Susan outside to meet her husband. Daniel and Tommy walked up from the corral just as they exited the cabin. Each man was carrying a rifle. They always liked to keep one handy, just in case.

Emily saw them and said, "Daniel, these are the Van Dusens. This is Charles and Susan. They are on their way to New Orleans."

Daniel asked, "Did you say Charles Van Dusan?"

Van Dusan reached out to shake Daniel's hand as he said, "Yes. Happy to make your acquaintance."

Daniel chose not to shake the man's hand. Instead, he raised his rifle and pointed it at Van Dusan. "Charles Van Dusan of New Orleans is one of the most notorious con men and murderers in the south. He's been known to take young rich wives, and gain access to their families' wealth. Then, they mysteriously die of unknown causes, or they have an accident. He is also known as Charles Vanderford and Charlie Ford. Tommy, point your rifle at those men."

Charlie Ford grew up in New Orleans, the son of a drunken father and a prostitute mother. He began a life of crime at an early age out of necessity. He was kicked out of the house at age twelve because there wasn't enough money to feed him and support his father's drinking or his mother's addiction to opium. He developed his skills at conning early in life. He found it exhilarating. He had a talent for making up stories to gain things he wanted or needed. He discovered that people were less likely to trust someone dressed like a vagrant. So, he found a way to make himself presentable. He always wore the best clothing he could get his hands on.

He married his first mark, only sixteen when he was twenty. Her father owned a hotel in the French Quarter called the Tres Jolie. Charlie, now known as Charles Vanderford, married Jocelyn after convincing her father that he was a well-to-do businessman in the export business. Her father, Jean Pierre Arnault, consented to the marriage and welcomed Charles into the family. Not long afterward, Arnault was killed in a robbery attempt in which the suspects were never identified.

Six months later, once the estate had been passed to Jocelyn, She too met with an untimely death, leaving everything to her husband. The estate was soon liquidated. The Arnault mansion and the Tres Jolie were sold. Once Vanderford had finished selling off the estate, he had nearly three hundred thousand dollars. The money, however, didn't last. Charles developed a gambling habit. He lost almost all of his newfound wealth in a matter of months. Then, he searched for his next target after changing his name to Charles Van Dusan.

Tommy did as Daniel instructed. Emily took the cue, reached into the cabin doorway, and produced a rifle. Daniel searched Van Dusan for weapons he might be carrying on his person. At the same time, Tommy and Emily pointed their guns at the other men. Daniel found a six-inch knife hidden in the waistband of Van Dusan's trousers and a small pistol inside his coat. Once Daniel was satisfied, the man was no longer armed; he instructed him, "Have a seat over there on the porch, and don't move."

Daniel searched each man for weapons. Once they were all cleared, Daniel tied them up with leather thongs. Van Dusan said, "You have no authority to hold us here. You are not the law."

Daniel replied, "You're right. I'm not the law. But the law just rode out of here this morning, and I know where they're headed."

Daniel left Emily and Tommy to guard the men while he saddled Hoss and rode up the ridge to find the militia. They had about an hour's head start, but he knew they wouldn't travel quickly. He galloped his horse in search of Crockett's troops.

Susan Van Dusan was in utter shock at the events. She couldn't believe the accusations that had been made against her husband. He seemed so refined and successful to her. However, she wondered why he had no transportation back home to New Orleans. He had arranged the carriage and two extra horses for his men with her father.

On the other hand, she had never been comfortable around his men. Although they were dressed in elegant suits, they never acted like gentlemen. They were uncouth and drank too much to suit her. She was beginning to feel that she had just been rescued from some eventual tragedy. This thought made her shudder in fear.

Amy wondered why Tommy had not shown up for lunch, so she walked to Emily's cabin to see what was happening. She saw people gathered around Emily's cabin and thought she was missing out on new visitors, so she walked more quickly. When she got closer, she realized four men were seated on the porch with their hands tied behind their backs. Tommy was pointing his rifle at them. A young woman was resting at the other end of the porch, sitting with Emily. "Tommy? What's happening here?"

Tommy replied, "Well, seems we've got us some outlaws here. Daniel's rode up tryin' to ketch up with the militia. We're holdin' em here till he gits back."

Emily said, "Amy, this is Susan. Would you mind sitting with her while I fix us all some lunch? She's had a bit of a start this morning."

Amy replied, "Sure. I'd be happy to."

Emily went inside and fried bacon, sliced tomatoes, and whipped up some fresh mayonnaise. She made sandwiches for everyone and then served them. Charles asked, "How are we supposed to eat with our hands tied behind us?"

Tommy tied their hands in front of them and took extra precautions by tying their feet together. To make things even more difficult to escape, he linked the men to one another so one couldn't move without everyone moving.

Emily served coffee as well. When everyone had finished eating, Van Dusan announced, "I need to go to the privy."

Tommy said, "Sorry, Mister. You ain't goin' nowheres til Daniel gits back."

Van Dusan raised his voice and demanded, "What am I supposed to do? I have to go to the outhouse!"

Emily answered, "You better figure out a way to hold it. Or don't. It's your pretty trousers."

Van Dusan was shouting now when he said, "Confound you, woman! I'm going to ..."

"You better lower your voice, Mr. Fancypants. You forget I know how to sew things shut. It would make me very happy to sew that trap of yours shut."

Van Dusan concentrated on holding his bladder rather than arguing with Emily.

Two hours later, Daniel rode back into the valley with five men. Crockett had sent Sergeant Clark and four of his militia to gather the wanted men and bring them to Lawrenceburg. Daniel said to Clark, "Here they are, Sergeant. The one on the left is Van Dusan."

Clark said, "Alright, men, let's get them ready for transport."

Van Dusan spoke up politely and asked, "May I please go to the privy, now?"

Clark responded, "Sure, Mister. Any of you other men need to go?"

They all murmured their reply, "*Yes.*"

Clark ordered, "Carter! Take these men to the outhouse one at a time. As they come back, we'll prepare them for transport."

Carter did as instructed. Then, Clark asked anyone listening, "Are these their horses?"

Susan spoke up and said, "No, Sir. They are mine."

"Who are you, miss?"

"I'm Susan Claiborne. I'm from Richmond, Virginia. Mr. Van Dusan married me under pretense. I'm beginning to realize that my life is in danger. These people have saved me.

Clark instructed, "Well, Miss Claiborne, you'll be expected to testify against these men. You'll need to stay here in Tennessee until the trial."

Emily spoke up, "She can stay with us."

Clark replied, "Alright, Mrs. Lane. The Colonel will send a rider when a court date is set."

"Thank you, Sergeant," Daniel said.

Once all the prisoners had relieved themselves, the militia strung them together behind one of the riders. Van Dusan asked, "Where are you taking us?"

Clark said, "Lawrenceburg. It's a fifty-mile walk, so we best get moving."

The militia towed the prisoners out of the valley and moved south. The climb up the ridge was slow, but they made it without losing anyone. They still had four hours of daylight left. Clark would try to make fifteen miles by nightfall.

Susan told Emily, "I don't want to put you out. Is there an inn somewhere nearby?"

Emily replied, "Don't be silly. You aren't putting us out. We can make you a bed in the back of the wagon if you don't mind."

"That will be fine. I really appreciate all you have done for me. I hate to think what might have happened to me had your husband not recognized Charles."

When Emily could talk to Daniel away from everyone else, she asked, "Won't this disturb the timeline or something? Haven't you changed the future by disturbing the past?"

Daniel smiled and said, "I used my knowledge of the past, yes. But I haven't changed the future. I just fulfilled it. Charles Van Dusan was arrested in Tennessee for his crimes. He was taken into custody by Crockett's militia after receiving information about him from a local resident. As it turned out, Crockett never named who that local resident was."

Emily rolled her eyes, shook her head, then walked away.

CHAPTER 20

Daniel was tired after the day's events. The long, fast ride had worn him out. As Emily read one of her medical books, Daniel picked up Gus's diary and began to read.

December 26, 1779

Yesterday was Christmas. I haven't seen my family for a little over six years now. I sure do miss them!

I heard a whippoorwill last night. I thought it strange to hear one this late in the year, but I'm sure I heard it. It reminded me of when I was a boy. Robbie and I went

camping one night down by the creek that ran through the Grove. I woke up early before the sun rose. I needed to pee. When I stepped outside to find a place, I heard it.

Whip-poor-will, whip-poor-will, it sang. Robbie heard it, too. That was the last time I ever heard one until last night.

Timothy and I spent most of yesterday sitting on a bluff overlooking the salt flats. It was Christmas Day, and we didn't feel like working much, so we sat there and talked. Around noon, some people started to show up on the flats. Men, maybe forty of them, came from the east and settled in on the salt flats. They started cutting down trees and began constructing a stockade.

In the middle of the afternoon, boats began to arrive on the Cumberland River. There were large boats and canoes and even pirogues. I counted 30 vessels in all. Men, women, and children all were arriving to build a settlement near the salt flats. Timothy decided we should go and see what they were up to.

December 25, 1779

Timothy and Gus descended the bluff from where they had been perched while watching the strangers enter their valley. Timothy was not a happy man. They were encroaching upon his best trapping and hunting grounds. He had worked in this area for many years, even before Gus came along.

Two men approached them as they walked down into the clearing where men were furiously working. "Hello! May I help you?" one of them asked.

With fire in his eyes and hatred on his breath, Timothy replied with a strong French accent, "Who are you people, and what are you doing here?"

The same man replied, "I'm James Robertson, and this is John Donelson. Who might you be?"

"My name is Demonbreun! What are you doing here?"

"We're here to build a settlement. We traveled here from the Watauga Valley in North Carolina. We plan to build a fort and homesteads for all of these people."

"No! You cannot!" shouted Timothy. "This area is mine. I have trapped here for over ten years. You cannot come in here and just claim it."

"We aren't just claiming it," Robertson said. "This land belongs to the Chickasaw, from what I understand, and they have struck a deal to allow us to settle here. The Chickasaw may have allowed you to trap here, but this is not your land."

Gus watched as they volleyed arguments back and forth. He knew Timothy could be an angry individual, but he had never seen him this volatile before. After much dispute and screaming in French on Timothy's part, the men separated. As Timothy turned and trudged away, Gus looked questioningly at the two men and reluctantly followed.

Once they had reached their camp, Timothy began tossing everything within his grasp. He threw tools into the air, slammed beaver traps down on the ground, knocked over the ironworks that held their cooking pot over the fire, and generally just threw a fit.

Gus kept his distance. He knew Timothy would eventually calm down so that it would be safe to speak to him. For now, he would stay away and try to find a quiet place to think.

Gus had spent the last six and a half years in this area in this century. He was now twenty-two years old. Gus didn't know much about history but recognized the names Donelson and Robertson. Just as he had recognized his friend's name, Demonbreun. Streets, bridges, and even towns were named after these men in the Nashville area. He had never spent much time in Nashville while growing up in the area. Still, he knew the names from watching the news on television with his family back in Summertown.

The next day, Gus and Timothy continued their daily routine of setting and checking traps along the Cumberland River. They also watched for the opportunity to kill the occasional bear, fox, or elk that might wander into the salt lick. Timothy was unusually quiet over the next few days and said little to Gus. Gus said little, back. He feared Timothy would begin another tantrum if he said something wrong, so he kept quiet.

After a week, they returned to the bluff where they had spotted the settlers initially. The immigrants had made good progress in building their fort. The outer wall was nearly finished, and they had almost completed a blockhouse at one corner of the structure. Timothy paused as he looked down into the valley. He let out a "*humph!*" then turned and walked away.

Gus was suddenly startled from sleep that night as an enormous explosion erupted. He rolled from his bedroll onto his feet, grabbed his rifle, and ran outside to see what was happening. Gus ran to the bluff and looked into the valley. He saw the blockhouse, and most of the north corner of the fort wall engulfed in flames.

Gus spotted men and women struggling to extinguish the flames by pouring buckets of water onto the fire. They worked at it for hours, passing buckets up and down the line from man to man when the buckets were full of water and from woman to woman when the buckets were empty. Gus climbed down the bluff and ran to aid the settlers. He found a place in line with the men as they passed the buckets down the line.

Smoke billowed around them all as the flames reached toward the stars. Ash floated through the air like snowflakes in winter. A large log from the structure's wall fell, nearly landing on top of two women carrying empty buckets back to the river. As the log hit the ground, a cloud of soot flew into the air, causing them to cough and choke. The wind picked up a bit, causing the smoke to dash toward the ground. Men and women choked as the black smoke filled their lungs.

Nevertheless, they continued fighting against the flames that consumed their new home. They worked throughout the early morning hours. The fire was finally out when the sun had risen above the trees. The north and west walls of the fort were nearly gone.

No one seemed to know how it began, and the settlers were all startled by the explosion. Gus meandered around the area, looking for clues as to how the fire had started. He noticed a burnt area on the ground outside of where the charred blockhouse once stood. A thin line of soot ran from the structure into the trees at the forest's edge.

Gus was pretty sure what had happened. Someone had poured a line of gunpowder from the forest's edge to the fort wall. They must have left a keg of gunpowder outside of the wall so it could catch fire. The barrel explosion caused the fort and blockhouse to catch fire and quickly burn.

"*Timothy*!" he whispered to himself.

Six of the men, being led by Robertson, approached Gus. "Thanks for your help, young man. I didn't catch your name before."

"My name is Gus. Gus Childers."

"Well, Gus, did your French friend have anything to do with this?" asked Robertson. "Did he say anything to you about his plans to sabotage our fort?"

Gus replied, "He hasn't said much of anything to me over the past week. Since you people showed up, he's been reticent, which, for Timothy, is very unusual. He normally talks non-stop from morning til night."

"Sounds like he snapped!" said Donelson as the other men murmured in agreement. Donelson continued, "Maybe we should go and have a talk with him now." Again, the men murmured in agreement.

Gus spoke up and said, "I think that might be a bad idea. Let me go and speak to him. He's less likely to pull a gun or knife on me as he would any of you. He's probably watching us all right now."

The men looked up and around, searching for any sign of someone spying on them. Gus said, "You've got plenty to keep you busy right here. I'll find him and speak to him."

As the men mumbled among themselves, Robertson finally spoke up and replied, "Alright. We'll wait. But if we don't hear from you soon, we'll come looking for both of you."

Gus nodded his head in understanding, then escaped into the forest.

Timothy had taught Gus how to be a pretty good tracker. But Gus knew that Timothy would not leave a trail for him to follow. So, he decided to look in the usual places for Timothy. Gus looked for him at the salt lick. Then, he moved up to the bluff, where Gus eventually returned to their camp. There, he found Timothy sitting by the fire, cleaning his rifle. Timothy never looked up to acknowledge Gus's arrival. He just asked, "Where have you been all morning?" Gus replied, "I've been looking for you."

Timothy said, "I have been right here, wondering where you had gone. I thought maybe you had left me to join those squatters."

Gus then asked, "Did you do it?"

"Do what?"

"Did you set fire to the fort?" Timothy sneered and replied, "I don't know what you are talking about."

"Sure you do," challenged Gus. "You had to have heard it. The explosion knocked me out of my bed. What do you have against those people? What have they done to you?"

Timothy responded, "They are trespassers. This is my land."

"No!" replied Gus. "This is not your land. Just because the Chickasaw have allowed you to hunt and trap here for these past years, doesn't make it yours. Besides, they haven't said you can't continue to hunt here. Leave them alone. Trap your furs. Trade with these men rather than fight them."

Timothy replied, "If you like them so much, why don't you join them?"

Gus replied, "I will. Timothy, you've helped me and taught me so much over the past six years. But I won't stay here if you can't get along with other people. There will be more coming. This is just the beginning. More and more people will be settling in this area. And you won't be able to stop them."

"Then, go!" said Timothy.

Gus gathered up his haversack with all of his personal belongings. He left his rifle since it wasn't *really* his anyway. As he started to go, he paused by the fire and turned to Timothy. He said, "Au revoir."

Then he turned back to the trail and left, never looking back. Gus never saw Timothy Demonbreun again.

Chapter 21

June 14, 1819

It was a rainy day. The stock still had to be looked after, but Daniel quickly worked on it. When he got to the corral, Daniel saw the horses and mules huddled underneath the big tree in the middle. Now, nine horses and two mules shared the same pen: Amy's horse, Daniel's three horses, Emily's mare, colt, and two mules, and Susan's three horses. The corral was getting crowded, so Daniel contemplated expanding the corral or maybe building an additional pen. Daniel admired Susan's stock. They were Morgan horses. Not overly large horses, but they were stout and strong.

As Daniel made his way back to the cabin, he stopped by the wagon where Susan was staying. "Susan?" he called out.

"Yes," she answered.

"Why don't you come into the cabin. It will be much dryer there. This rain looks like it might be here for a while."

Susan replied, "Are you sure you don't mind? I wouldn't want to put anyone out."

"Not at all," said Daniel. "Emily would love to have another woman to talk to."

Susan pulled a blanket over her head and stepped down from the wagon with the help of Daniel. He escorted her to the cabin and opened the door. Emily was cooking breakfast when they walked in. "Susan! Come in and dry yourself. I'll have some breakfast ready soon."

They all leisurely ate their breakfast. Jake sat under the table, waiting for something to fall to the floor that he might find tasty. Shortly after breakfast, the rain began to let up. Jake lifted his head and gave a *"woof,"* indicating that he had heard something outside. Daniel went to the door and opened it. Jake was right on Daniel's heels. As soon as Jake stuck his nose out of the doorway, he began to bark. Someone was riding down into the valley, just the other side of the Beaver. "Hush, Jake!" said Daniel.

Daniel recognized one of the riders. It was Sergeant Clark of the militia. Daniel stepped onto the porch to greet the men as they rode up to the cabin. Emily and Susan walked out to see who it was. "Good morning, Sergeant!" said Daniel. "I didn't expect to see you back so soon. What brings you here?"

"Mornin', Daniel. Colonel Crockett sent me. He needs Mrs. Van Dusan to come back with me to Lawrenceburg. He has sent word to New Orleans about her husband, and they plan to extradite him back there. They need her to go down there as a witness. The Louisiana attorney general is sending men to pick them up and transport them back to New Orleans."

Susan looked at Emily with a frightful look. She didn't want to go to New Orleans. Especially with men she didn't know. Emily recognized Susan's fear and told her, "Don't worry. Daniel will take care of you."

Daniel asked the sergeant, "When do we need to leave?"

"We?" asked the sergeant. "Are you planning on going also?"

"I am. Wherever Miss Claiborne goes, I'll be going."

"Daniel, you know we're more than capable of escorting this young lady to Lawrenceburg. There's no need for you to come along."

Daniel replied, "I trust you and your men. It's what might happen after she leaves your protection that concerns me."

"Do you mean to escort her all the way to New Orleans?"

"I'll be escorting her as far as I deem it necessary to ensure her protection."

Sergeant Clark replied, "Well, alright, then. We should leave as soon as possible."

Daniel looked at Emily and waited for her nod of approval. She looked at him with pride and nodded to him. Emily knew she could count on Daniel to do what was right in helping those who weren't capable of protecting themselves. Daniel went to the corral and hitched up one of Susan's Morgan horses to her carriage. The carriage would be a more comfortable mode of transportation for her and would also carry her luggage. Daniel drove the wagon to the front of the cabin, where the sergeant and the other rider were waiting.

Daniel got out, loaded Susan's luggage into the back, and helped her into the front seat so she could ride next to him. He then went inside and geared up for the trip. Daniel draped two braces with pistols over his shoulders. He gathered his powder horns and shot bag, his tomahawk, and two rifles, then carried them out to the carriage.

Sergeant Clark asked, "Are you expecting trouble?"

Daniel replied, "Pray for the best, but expect the worst."

Daniel walked over to Emily to kiss her goodbye and whispered to her, "I should be back within a week."

Emily looked into his eyes and said, "You know something, don't you."

Daniel winked at her, returned to the carriage, and stepped into it.

Susan waved to Emily and said, "Thank you, Emily, for everything."

Emily replied, "Stay safe. Do everything Daniel tells you to."

Daniel looked at Jake and said, "Jake, stay here!"

Jake reluctantly and disappointedly obeyed his master. Daniel turned the Morgan and drove them through the Beaver and up the hill that led to the Gordon's stand. It was still raining, but not as hard now. The sergeant set a steady pace, trotting his horse along the trail. He hoped to make Sheboss Stand by dusk.

They rode into the Gordon's stand around three o'clock. They watered the horses and stretched their legs a bit before continuing on. Dolly came out of the house to greet them. "Howdy, Daniel."

Dolly looked around as if she had expected someone or something else to be riding up with them. Daniel asked, "Are you looking for something, Dolly?"

"No, I was just checking to see if you brought another body with you."

Daniel smiled at her joke, stepped down from the carriage, and hugged her. "How's the captain?"

Dolly replied, "He seems to be getting weaker every day. I'm getting really concerned about him. He just hasn't been himself since he returned from Florida."

Daniel said, "If you'd like Emily to have another look at him, just send one of the boys over to fetch her."

Dolly responded, "Well, I may do that. We'll see how he feels tomorrow."

Sergeant Clark suggested, "We best get going. Are you ready?"

Daniel replied, "Sure thing."

They all mounted their rides and rode toward the ferry crossing. They found young Tom and a new man running the ferry when they arrived. "Howdy, Daniel!" called Tom. "Good to see you again."

"Hi, Tom. I see you've got a new partner."

"This here's Ben. He just started last week."

Daniel looked the man over. He appeared to be in his mid-twenties. Ben wore a scraggly beard, and his eyes were the palest blue Daniel had ever seen. He wore typical frontier garb, but his trousers must have been a little too big because the young man was always pulling them up. Ben wasn't using his hands to pull up his pants. He seemed to have a habit, or maybe it was a tick that caused him to pull his pants up by using the inside of his forearms. He would continuously place his arms against the waistband of his pants, then shrug his shoulders, trying to lift his pants up to a more comfortable position. It was one of the strangest things Daniel had ever seen.

Everyone rode onto the barge that would carry them across the Duck. Once they were all situated, Tom and Ben began pulling the ropes to move them across the river to the other side. Once on the other side, Daniel handed Tom two dollars. "We don't usually charge the militia for crossing, Daniel," he said.

"That's okay," Daniel said. "I've got you covered anyway. You and Ben can split it."

"Thanks Daniel!" Tom said. "That's mighty generous of you."

Sergeant Clark led the way as they trotted down the trail toward Sheboss Stand. The rain had stopped falling, although drops of water still fell upon them from the wet branches of the trees that hovered over the trail. The carriage canopy kept Daniel and Susan reasonably dry, but the riders were pretty well soaked. Their frontier garb helped to protect against the elements, but it would not keep them completely dry.

The trail was a mucky mess. So much rain had made it difficult to travel. A ride that would have usually taken about four or five hours turned into a six-and-a-half-hour ride. Because of the dark cloud cover, the skies darkened much earlier than usual in June. They rode the last hour in hazy dusk. At eight o'clock that evening, they finally rode into the clearing of Sheboss Stand.

David came out of the cabin when he heard riders approaching. His face lit up when he realized that Daniel was among the riders. He raised his hand in greeting and called out to Daniel, "Hallito, Nafkl!"

Daniel stepped down from the carriage and embraced his Chickasaw brother. "It's good to see you, Nafkl. How are Sarah and the baby?"

David responded, "They are good."

Just then, Sarah walked out of the cabin to see who had ridden into their stand. When she saw Daniel, she rushed to him and hugged him. "Oh, Daniel! It's so good to see you. Is Emily with you?"

Daniel replied, "No, she couldn't come this time. Sarah, this is Susan Claiborne. We are escorting her to Lawrenceburg to meet with Colonel Crockett about a legal matter. She needs a dry place to sleep tonight."

Sarah replied, "Well, of course. We'll get her set up in the cabin. I hope you and the other men don't mind sleeping in the barn tonight."

Daniel said, "No, that will be just fine. What's that on your back?"

Sarah was carrying her new baby boy strapped to her back like an Indian woman would carry her papoose. Sarah smiled and turned her back to Daniel as she replied, "This is little Daniel. We call him Danny."

Daniel grabbed the little guy's hand and said, "Well, hey there, little guy. How old is he now?"

Sarah said, "He'll be seven months in just a couple of days. He's already a handful. He sure loves his Poppa."

Daniel smiled as he turned back to Susan and said, "Let's get you settled in for the night."

He unloaded Susan's gear and took it into the spare cabin. He lit a lamp for her and then stepped out to tend to the horse and carriage. Sarah checked in on Susan to see if she might be hungry. Susan denied any nourishment. She was simply tired and wanted to sleep. So, Sarah left her.

The weather cleared overnight to clear skies and sunshine the next morning. The riders felt refreshed after their sleep. As soon as the men woke, they prepared their horses for the journey that still lay ahead of them. If the trail wasn't too bad, they would make it to Lawrenceburg by noon.

They led their horses and the carriage up to the cabin, where they found Sarah setting out a bountiful breakfast for them. She had made biscuits, fried bacon, and eggs, and she served fried apples for a little extra treat. Everyone ate their fill, gobbling down the food as if they were starving. Afterward, Daniel loaded Susan's gear back onto the carriage so they could get started down the trail.

The trail was still muddy, but it was passable. Once in a while, the Morgan would lose his footing and slip, throwing clumps of mud in Daniel and Susan's direction. Susan's beautiful clothing was spattered with brown spots of wet dirt. Whenever they found a relatively dry patch of ground, the wheels of the carriage would throw mud at them as they cleared themselves of the wet muck.

They rode past the turnoff that led to Grinder's Stand. Susan asked, "Should we stop here and rest a bit?"

Daniel replied, "No, we'll be in Lawrenceburg soon. Besides, the woman who owns that stand has a history with me."

Susan asked, "Oh? What kind of history, if you don't mind my asking?"

Daniel explained, "She hit me over the back of my head with a club once. I'd be dead if Colonel Crockett and his men hadn't come along when they did."

"Why did she hit you?"

Daniel said, "Well, she thought I stole a horse from a friend of hers. He was an evil cuss that attacked Sarah Colbert about a year ago. He and three other men attacked Sheboss. I had seen the men on the trail and decided to go back to Sheboss just in case they became a problem. When they attacked Sarah and David, David and I killed them all. We split up their gear, and I happened to get the Sorrel that Prissy's friend was riding. When she found out her friend was dead and I had something to do with it, she clubbed me when I wasn't expecting it."

Susan replied, "My! The frontier is quite uncivilized, isn't it? I had no idea things were so wild here. Your friend back there at the stand was the first Indian I have ever seen."

Daniel said, "Really? Well, David Colbert is a very civil man. He is one person you don't have to worry about as long as you treat him and his family well. It's the white man that you have to be suspicious of here."

Susan stated, "You mean like Charles."

Daniel replied, "That I do. But others like him as well."

Another hour down the trail found the small caravan riding into Lawrenceburg. It was a small community of about six hundred. They found Crockett at his home that sat next to a creek. There were three other buildings on the farm. Crockett was a businessman as well as the leader of the militia. His wife ran most of the businesses. Crockett was usually unavailable to run them because of his duties as the militia commander as well as the local magistrate. There was a water wheel on the side of one of the buildings on the Crockett property. The waterwheel rotated in the rushing waters of the creek, turning the millstones within the building. Along with the gristmill was a still where whiskey was produced and another building where gunpowder was manufactured.

Crockett came out of the house as they rode up. He was a little surprised to see Daniel driving the carriage. "Well, Daniel. What brings you to my neck of the woods?"

"I'm here to escort Miss Claiborne to ensure her safety."

Crockett asked, "Miss Claiborne?"

Daniel replied, "It's her maiden name. The name that she prefers, under the present circumstances."

"I see. Well, Miss Claiborne, won't you step down?"

Daniel got out of the carriage and moved to Susan's side of the carriage to help her down. He then escorted her over to meet the Colonel.

Crockett shook her hand and then said, "We're expecting the authorities from New Orleans to arrive later today. We'll try to get things moving along so you can be on your way to New Orleans tomorrow. Mrs. Crockett has set up a guest room for you to spend the night. Daniel, you're welcome to put up in the barn if you like."

Daniel replied, "That will be fine."

After Daniel unloaded Susan's gear and placed it in her room, he unhitched the Morgan and put him in a corral with some of Crockett's horses. Later in the afternoon, after Susan had rested, she met Daniel outside. They took a stroll around the Crockett estate going through the various buildings, watching the workers as they performed their assigned tasks. When they approached the whiskey still, Susan became a little sick to her stomach, and her head ached from the odors of the souring grain. Daniel quickly escorted her away from the smell to relieve her unwanted symptoms.

Just before dusk, two men rode into the Crockett farm. They both wore suits that were by no means expensive or well-kept. They were tattered, in fact, and thread-barren. Not what Daniel expected to see from men representing law enforcement in New Orleans. The two dismounted in front of Crockett and Daniel, and one of them said, "Colonel Crockett, I'm Pierre Boudreau. I'm a deputy marshal for the city of New Orleans sent to collect some prisoners. This here is deputy marshal Kent Wade".

The man spoke with a strong Southern accent. Daniel was immediately suspicious of him. With a name like Boudreau, Daniel had expected a strong French or at least a Cajun accent.

Boudreau presented Crockett with a set of papers introducing the men to him and requesting that the extradition of the prisoners be fulfilled. Davy looked over the papers and verified that the prisoners were to be turned over to marshals Boudreau and Wade for transport back to New

Orleans. They also extended a request to have the crucial witness in the crime accompany the marshals back to New Orleans to testify against the accused.

The Colonel said, "Everything seems to be in order. Your prisoners are being held in the jail in town. We'll turn them over to you in the morning. Miss Claiborne is your witness. She will be traveling with you. We'll have her in town tomorrow morning at seven o'clock."

Daniel interrupted, "I'll be going too."

Davy then said, "Gentlemen, this is Daniel Lane. He will be traveling with Miss Claiborne as she travels to New Orleans."

Daniel reached out to shake Boudreau's hand and said, "Comment allez-vous?"

Boudreau responded, "Huh? What was that?"

Daniel then said, "Nice to meet you, gentlemen."

The man failed Daniel's test. Even the most uneducated man in New Orleans would have recognized the French phrase that Daniel had used. These men were not marshals.

Then, the two men excused themselves and rode back to town to find lodging for the night. After they left, Daniel took Davy aside and spoke to him privately. He didn't want Susan to be uneasy about her situation. At least no more than she already was. Daniel told Crockett, "Those men aren't marshals."

Davy asked, "What makes you say that?"

Daniel replied, "Well, first of all, they don't look the part. Their clothing is more that of saddle tramps or outlaws. Secondly, Boudreau is a French name, but he didn't understand when I spoke French to him. Even the most ignorant of individuals in New Orleans would understand the phrase, comment alley-vous. Thirdly, I know the history of Charles Van

Dusan. I know that he tried to escape custody during extradition from Tennessee."

Crockett then asked, "What do you propose I do, then?"

Daniel suggested, "Why don't you send a few of your men to travel with us. They might be less likely to try something if they know they're outnumbered."

Crockett said, "I'll get word out to some of the men. I'll ask for volunteers. I won't order anyone to go with you, though. If no one shows up, you'll be on your own."

Daniel replied, "I understand. Thanks."

The next morning, Daniel and Susan loaded up the carriage and drove to town to meet the group traveling to New Orleans. Daniel pulled up at the jail just as Boudreau and Wade were bringing out the four prisoners. When Van Dusan saw Daniel and his wife drive up, he sneered and mumbled under his breath. Just as they all got ready to leave, Sergeant Clark and another man rode up to join them. Daniel recognized the other man as Billy Johnson. He usually served as an orderly with Doc Simmons in the militia. Billy was very young, maybe only sixteen. He was green as a soldier. Daniel had his doubts about his ability to be of help in a fight. Daniel greeted them, "Sergeant, Billy, thanks for coming."

The sergeant replied, "Sorry we couldn't find more to come along. Most of the men have crops to bring in."

Daniel replied, "I understand."

Boudreau then announced, "Let's get moving. New Orleans is a fer piece to go."

They all followed behind him, Boudreau in the lead, the prisoners and Wade behind them, and then the carriage. Clark and Johnson brought up the rear. They rode back to the Natchez Trail, moving west. Once they found the trail, they turned south toward Alabama. They would ride the trail for forty miles until they reached the Tennessee River. Then, they would cross the river by using the Colbert Ferry.

Chief George Colbert was the brother of Chief William Colbert. George owned and operated the ferry that crossed the Tennessee River as well as a stand nearby the river in Alabama. Chief George was also a farmer who owned over one hundred fifty slaves and managed the corn and cotton grown there. Chickasaw George, as he was known, was a shrewd businessman. Daniel once read where George had charged General Andrew Jackson seventy-five thousand dollars to take his soldiers and their horses across the river after the battle of New Orleans. Daniel was never able to verify the information or discover where that funding came from for that crossing.

Forty miles was too far to travel in one day. Especially in the condition in which the trail would probably be after the significant rain they had recently had. Daniel noticed that Van Dusan rode closely to Boudreau, often even riding next to him. The two seemed to be in constant conversation together. Occasionally, Van Dusan would look over his shoulder at Susan as she rode next to Daniel in the carriage.

They decided to make camp at the Alabama and Tennessee border, thirty miles from where they had begun that morning. A small branch provided an ideal spot to sleep for the night. As darkness fell, everyone began to settle into their bedrolls.

Daniel pulled Clark aside and suggested, "Let's set up a watch in three-hour shifts. But don't let anyone know what we're doing. Make it seem like we're all bedding down for the night. I'll take the first watch."

Clark responded, "Fine. Wake Billy up at midnight. I'll take the third watch."

Daniel set up his and Susan's bedrolls on the far side of the carriage from Boudreau and the other men. He wanted the carriage to act as a barrier between them if something occurred during the night. A small fire was lit in the camp, and Boudreau and the other men set up their bedrolls around it. Daniel was thankful for the fire. He knew that it would illuminate the men sleeping around it yet make it difficult to see anything outside of their inner circle.

Once Daniel got Susan settled in for the night, he secretly set up a post behind a large Hickory tree. He sat against the tree, facing the fire. Those who sat near the fire couldn't see him. They could only assume that Daniel's group had all bedded down for the night.

All was quiet during Daniel's shift. At midnight, he woke Billy to quietly take his place by the tree. Daniel then slipped into his bedroll next to Susan's. Just as he settled in, he heard two western screech owls calling to each other. They sounded like a troop of monkeys chattering in the jungle. After five minutes or so, they settled down and were quiet. Daniel found it difficult to sleep. He wasn't sure whether or not to trust Billy as a night watchman. But slowly, Daniel drifted off to sleep.

Around five o'clock, Clark witnessed some stirring around the fire area. Boudreau and Wade were cutting away the bindings of the four prisoner's wrists. He saw that once Van Dusan had been freed, he picked up a rifle and began marching toward Susan.

Clark crawled over to Daniel and nudged his foot to awaken him. When Daniel stirred, he looked at Clark. Clark raised his forefinger to his lips to quiet Daniel, then pointed toward Van Dusan. Boudreau was struggling with Van Dusan, trying to keep him away from the others. He realized that Charles intended to kill Susan and anyone else who happened to get in his way. Van Dusan shook himself free of Boudreau's grasp and headed directly toward Susan.

It was still dark and difficult to see, but Charles raised his rifle as he moved toward the carriage and Susan. He cocked the gun and aimed where he thought she might be sleeping. Just as he pulled the trigger, Clark grabbed Susan's ankles and dragged her out of harm's way with a quick tug. The gun fired, and dirt flew in the air where the bullet struck.

The gunshot woke Billy, who tripped over his bedroll, trying to get to his feet. Daniel leaped from the ground into concealment behind the carriage. He reached into the carriage and retrieved his two pistols and his second rifle. Chaos erupted as everyone began firing at Daniel and his group. Susan lay on the ground next to the tree, shaking with fear. Daniel fired and hit Van Dusan in the shoulder, knocking him to the ground. Billy fired his rifle, missing everything. Clark fired, hitting one of Van Dusan's men in the chest. As Billy and Clark began reloading, Daniel was firing his second, third, and fourth shots. His second rifle shot hit Wade in the throat. Then, his first pistol shot struck Boudreau in the hip as he began to duck for cover. Van Dusan managed to reload and raised his rifle to aim while sitting on the ground. Daniel's second pistol shot hit him in the head. As the bullet struck him, Van Dusan pulled his own trigger, but his shot went wide of Daniel and hit Billy in the chest. Clark was able to reload and fired at the carriage driver and killed him. Daniel reloaded one of his pistols and then looked for a target. There was none. Van Dusan's last man and Boudreau escaped into the trees.

When the smoke cleared, five bodies lay dead on the ground: Billy and the other four men. Susan was in utter shock. Daniel went to her and lifted her from the ground. He helped her step up into the carriage where she could be more comfortable. Clark and Daniel then packed up the camp. There would be no more need to travel to New Orleans. They draped the bodies over the backs of five horses and tethered them together behind the carriage. Daniel led the way down the trail while Clark brought up the rear just in case the remaining fugitives came back after them.

They arrived back in Lawrenceburg shortly after six o'clock. Susan hadn't said a word the whole time they traveled that day. She finally spoke up as Daniel stopped the carriage in front of the jail. "I'd be dead now if you hadn't been there. I saw the look in Charles's eyes. He was going to kill me. How did you know?"

Daniel replied, "I knew of his reputation. I knew he was a con artist and a murderer. I wasn't about to let you fall prey to him."

Susan asked, "But how did you know he would escape?"

Daniel said, "He didn't escape. Boudreau and Wade were not who they said they were. In fact, Boudreau and Wade weren't their real names. They probably bushwacked the real marshals and took the paperwork for Charles's extradition from them."

Susan persisted, "Okay, but how did you know?"

Daniel answered, "I can't explain it. I just have a sense for these things."

Susan thought for a moment, then responded. "I think you're a prophet. I think God told you what to do. He sent you to help me, didn't he?"

Daniel smiled and said nothing.

CHAPTER 22

June 17, 1819

The day started like most days in the Water Valley, with everyone tending to their various chores. Tommy looked after the livestock and checked on the cornfield since Daniel had not yet returned. Emily and Amy made butter, baked it, and did the laundry. The chores on their little homestead were never-ending, but they all loved them. Emily and Daniel were especially happy in their circumstance. Daniel had always dreamed of living a simpler life and living it to the fullest. He and Emily were finally fulfilling that dream.

Shortly after noon, a rider came into the valley and crossed the Beaver Branch. Tommy, Amy, and Emily went into the front yard of Daniel and Emily's cabin to see who it was. It was Micah Gordon, Amy's brother. He wore a somber look on his face as he rode directly up to Amy and dismounted. "What is it, Micah?" she asked.

"It's Father," he said. "Father died yesterday. Mother asked me to come and get you. Luke and Mark are riding to Nashville to tell the others."

Tears filled Amy's eyes. She turned to Tommy for comfort, who held her in his arms tightly. Emily said, "Tommy, take her back to your cabin so she can get her things together. Micah and I can saddle up your horses for you."

After they finished saddling the horses, Emily said, "Micah, come inside, and I'll fix you some lunch. You can rest a spell before you ride back home with Amy and Tommy."

An hour later, Tommy and Amy walked back to Daniel and Emily's cabin to join up with Micah. As they all prepared to ride back up the trail, Emily told Amy, "Stay as long as you need to. I can handle things here just fine until you get back. Spend time with your family and give my love to your mother."

Amy replied, "I will. Thanks, Emily."

The three of them rode up the hill away from the Water Valley. Micah rode slightly ahead of Tommy and Amy. Tommy was usually not conversive, but he took Amy by the hand and said, "Tell me about your father."

Amy told him, "Well, you know he was a captain serving under General Jackson. He was always kind to me. I loved him dearly, but I also hated him. Well, not him but what he did. I hated that he always had to be away. He left an awful burden on Mother. She was always expected to take care of all of us and Father's businesses too. I don't remember it. It was before I was born. But, Mother said things were better when Father was Postmaster in Nashville because he was always home, then. They had a lovely plantation just outside of Nashville. Fifteen-hundred acres mother said. But he had to sell it all off when things got bad. Father owed some men a lot of money, although I'm not sure why. That's when they moved out here to the ferry crossing."

Tommy thought momentarily, then offered, "Well, I'm glad I got to meet him. And I'm glad he was able to see you get married. He looked very proud of you that day."

Amy squeezed Tommy's hand and smiled at his thoughts. She was happy she had found a husband who was so sensitive to her needs. They talked the whole way as they rode along the trail. Time passed quickly. Before they knew it, they had arrived at Amy's old home. Amy had cried a few tears along the way, but when she saw her mother coming out to meet her, she lost it. Tears flowed like the Duck between the two of them. They embraced and held onto one another for a very long time. Finally, Amy asked, "Where is he?"

Dolly said, "We've laid him out in the parlor. Come on. I'll go with you."

As Amy and Dolly entered the parlor, Amy found Lucy in the corner weeping for their father. Lucy saw Amy and quickly rose to greet her. They embraced, and the crying began all over again. Micah and Tommy entered the house, and Tommy timidly moved to be next to Amy as she stood next to her father's body.

Captain John Gordon was laid out on a table covered in a white cloth. Two flags were displayed in the room, hanging on standards, one on each side of the fireplace. The United States flag was on the right, while the Tennessee state flag was on the left. He wore his best dress military uniform. All of his medals and ribbons were displayed on the breast of his jacket. His hands were crossed at his waist, holding his saber. His hair and beard were trimmed perfectly, although his face was drawn and wrinkled. He had aged rapidly in his final months of life. Although he was only fifty-six, he looked to be seventy-six.

After a while, Amy turned to her mother and asked, "What of Belinda and Cynthia?"

Dolly replied, "They should be here tomorrow. Luke and Mark have gone to fetch them. Come on. Let me fix you something to eat. You must be starving after that long ride."

They followed Dolly to the next room, where she had prepared food for those who needed it. She had a roasted ham, potatoes, roasted corn, and much more. Very little of it had been touched. Understandably, almost everyone didn't feel like eating. Tommy and Amy fixed a plate for themselves. Tommy ate while Amy just picked at her food a little.

At noon the next day, a large caravan of riders and carriages drove into the farm. Everyone came out of the house and from all over the farm to see the spectacle. Cavalry riders, holding military company flags, the United States flag, and the Tennessee state flag, rode in columns of two. They were followed by military officers who seemed to be of great importance. Then came several carriages carrying many well-dressed people, followed by another column of cavalry riders.

Dolly recognized one of the officers right away. She also saw her two daughters, Belinda and Cynthia, and their families riding in the carriages. She met her family as they came to a halt, and more tears began to flow as they hugged one another. Amy and Lucy came out to greet the sisters, as well. All of the Gordon family members were together, hugging and greeting each other.

Orders came from an unknown voice to dismount. All military personnel dismounted their horses and fell into ranks to honor the Gordon family. An older gentleman in uniform walked over to meet Dolly and her family. It was the officer that Dolly had recognized as they rode into the farm. "General Jackson!" she cried out. "I didn't expect to see you here today."

"Dolly, you know better than to call me General. It's Andy to you."

"What are you doing here?" she asked.

"I just happened to be at the Hermitage yesterday, taking a short break from duties, when one of my officers delivered word that John had passed. I instructed them to put together an escort for your family to come home for the funeral. I intend Captain Gordon to be buried with full military honors, with your permission."

"Why, yes!" said Dolly. "I'm sure John would have loved that. He thought so highly of you."

Dolly invited the general and the family to all come into the parlor to pay their respects to Captain Gordon. General Jackson went in first and admired his friend, who lay so still in his dress uniform. He did not linger, knowing that so much of the family had not yet visited their lost family patriarch. All ten of the remaining Gordon children, with their spouses and children, gathered with Dolly in the parlor to say goodbye to their father.

Titus, the foreman for the Gordon estate, quietly walked into the parlor and looked at Dolly until he got her attention. She came to him and asked, "Yes?"

Titus said, "Miss Dolly, it's ready."

Dolly replied, "Have the boys bring it in, please."

Titus temporarily exited the house but returned with two of the slave men who were carrying a freshly built casket for the captain. The casket was beautifully made from Walnut. They sanded it to a smooth finish and then rubbed it with linseed oil. One of the slaves decorated it with wrought iron hardware and handles. It was indeed made with exceptional craftsmanship. Before they brought it into the parlor, Dolly asked everyone to step outside. Once everyone had left, Dolly, Titus, and the two slaves brought the casket into the room and placed the captain's body inside. After they put his body into the coffin, Dolly said one last goodbye, closed the lid to the casket, and latched it. They then draped the American flag over the top of the casket.

Dolly asked all of her sons to come back into the parlor. She instructed them that they would be pallbearers and had them lift the casket to carry it outside. Once outside, the sons lined up with coffin in hand. The rest of the family fell into procession behind the coffin. The General and his staff came next. Off to one side was a color guard and rifle corp standing at attention. With them was a corporal named Bridger. Bridger served as the company bugler. He blew the tune of **Amazing Grace** while the procession slowly walked to the family cemetery. When they reached the cemetery, the pallbearers set the casket down onto boards that lay across the opening of the grave where Captain Gordon's body would rest. The family gathered around the cemetery to hear the eulogy.

General Jackson stood before all who were present and spoke these words:

"It is with a heavy heart that I come before you all today to speak words that honor our loved one, Captain John Gordon, a man whom I have held in high regard for many years. He has served under me in many battles against our enemy. He was a man of truth, honor, and courage.

A loving husband to Dolly, father to eleven children, and grandfather. He was a soldier, a pioneer, an Indian trader, a farmer, and a businessman, and he served as Postmaster in Nashville for a time. Everyone who knew Captain Gordon had great respect for him. Not only was he an excellent officer in the military under my command, but he was also one of my closest friends. I will miss him, as I know you will also.

So now, O Lord, we present to you the soul of our brother John Gordon into your hands for safekeeping until we all meet again in the hereafter."

Then General Jackson began to recite the twenty-third Psalm, and everyone joined in with him.

"The Lord is my shepherd; I shall not want.

He maketh me to lie down in green pastures: he leadeth me beside the still waters.

He restoreth my soul: he leadeth me in the paths of righteousness for his name's sake.

Yea, though I walk through the valley of the shadow of death, I will fear no evil: for thou art with me; thy rod and thy staff they comfort me.

Thou preparest a table before me in the presence of mine enemies: thou anointest my head with oil; my cup runneth over.

Surely goodness and mercy shall follow me all the days of my life: and I will dwell in the house of the Lord forever. Amen!"

After the recitation, Jackson nodded at his captain of the guard. The captain marched his rifle corp into position close by and called the orders for a gun salute. At his request, five riflemen fired their weapons into the air. Immediately afterward,

Corporal Bridger played ***Blest Be the Tie That Binds*.**"

CHAPTER 23

June 19, 1819

The ride to Lawrenceburg seemed even more difficult on the way back. More rain fell, causing bogs along the trail. The carriage became stuck in the mud several times. Sergeant Clark, Daniel, and Susan took two days to make it back to Lawrenceburg rather than the one day it took them to come through the previous day.

A little after midday, they finally rode into the small town where their journey had begun. Colonel Crockett met them as they rode up to the courthouse. The three of them were all covered in mud and were weary from the journey. Crockett eyed the string of five horses that followed the carriage. Sergeant Clark rode up to him and said, "Billy's dead."

Crockett shook his head with disappointment. He turned to a young man beside him and said, "Tad, you better go and fetch Billy's Ma."

The young man was about thirteen. He ran through the dirt streets toward a group of houses on the south side of town. Then Crockett turned back to Clark and asked, "What happened?"

Clark responded, "We set up camp about thirty miles down the trail on the first night. Turns out, those marshals weren't marshals after all. They must have killed the real marshals and took their place. Daniel was suspicious of them, so he had us post a watch, away from the others. Turns out he was right. Just before dawn, the one called Boudreau cut the prisoners free. When Van Dusan got free, he grabbed up a gun and headed right for Miss Claiborne. He tried to kill her, but I pulled her out of the way of his shot. Then, all hell broke loose. Two of them got away. We brought the rest back with us."

Billy's Ma came running toward them. Tears were streaming down her face. "Where is he? Where's my Billy?"

Daniel and Clark walked over to Billy's horse and cut Billy's body loose from the saddle. They cradled his body in their arms and lay him on the porch in front of the courthouse. Mrs. Johnson wailed and wept while holding her son's head in her arms.

Crockett turned to the men who had gathered to see what was happening and said, "Men, let's get the rest of these bodies put into the dirt. We'll also need to dig a proper grave for Billy in their family cemetery."

Everyone scattered, doing just as the colonel instructed. Colonel Crockett, Daniel, and Susan rode back to Crockett's farm, where they would stay the night.

Daniel and Susan packed up the next morning and began the trip back home. Daniel hoped they could make it to the Gordon stand by nightfall. He realized Sarah and David Colbert would want them to stay at Sheboss for the night, but he wanted to get home to see Emily.

The trail between Lawrenceburg and the Duck River was in much better shape than what they had traveled through down south. Susan's Morgan horse had little trouble moving down the trail. They arrived at Sheboss around noon, and Sarah talked them into staying for lunch. But, after they finished eating, they were back on the trail. Five hours later, they pulled into Gordon's Stand.

Daniel was surprised to see Tommy and Amy there. Then he remembered the date—Captain Gordon was dead. Tommy walked up to the carriage as it pulled in. He looked at Daniel and said, "Amy's Pa died a couple of days ago. We buried him yesterday."

Tommy then realized that Daniel was not surprised by the news. He took Daniel aside and spoke to him in a low voice. "You already knew it, didn't ya?"

Daniel only said, "I'm sorry for their loss."

Tommy asked, "Why didn't you let me know before? Maybe there was something we could have done for him. Maybe Emily could have kept him alive?"

Daniel replied, "Tommy, that's not the way this works. We can't change things just because it might make a loved one feel less hurt. There is a timeline. If we change that timeline, it could change history. We have to be careful about such things."

Tommy asked, "Well, what about Susan? Wasn't she suppose to go to New Orleans? What's she doing back here?"

Daniel answered, "She was supposed to go toward New Orleans. But she never made it there. Her husband planned an escape along the way. I went along with her because I needed to make sure the timeline didn't change. If he had been successful, then she might be dead now. And that could change everything in the future. I knew Van Dusan would be killed trying to escape. I just wanted to make sure Susan didn't lose her life in the process."

Tommy said, "I don't know if I agree with all this. Who's to say we haven't already changed the timeline?"

Daniel said, "We don't know for sure. But we can't purposefully change things to go the way we want them to. I've studied our history. I know what is supposed to happen. I will do my best to steer things in the right direction without regard to what I selfishly want. It would be best if you didn't concern yourself with what might happen in the future. You'll be a lot happier if you just live day to day with your new wife. Make her happy. Be happy. Don't worry about tomorrow."

Emily and Jake moped around the homestead, waiting for Daniel, Tommy, and Amy to return home. The day was muggy and unbearably hot. She and Jake sat on the front porch as she used a dish towel to keep the sweat wiped from her face and neck. She considered walking down to the Beaver and taking her shoes off. The thought of dipping her bare feet into the cold water was enticing. After several minutes, she decided she would do just that. She said, "Come on, Jake!"

The two of them stepped down from the porch and walked toward the flowing waters of the Beaver Branch. They didn't get twenty feet from the cabin when Jake started barking. He had turned his attention toward the bluff and hill that rested behind her cabin. Six horses and two riders came trotting in from the southeast. Emily knew right away that they were Indians. She turned and returned to the cabin and retrieved a rifle from inside the doorway. Then, she walked out behind the house to meet the riders.

Emily cradled the rifle in her arms in a manner that would be non-threatening to the riders. She wanted to be safe, but she didn't want to be unwelcoming. Two young men between the ages of fifteen and twenty, she thought, were leading a string of four Indian ponies. She smiled as they approached and said, "Hello!"

The older of the two was very much what she would expect of a member of one of the Indian nations. His hair was long and black, his skin was tanned and smooth, and his eyes were brown. The other young man was very different. His skin was lighter. His hair was long but blonde, and his eyes were blue. As they greeted Emily, it was he who spoke. "Hello. Are you Shobohli Eho?"

Emily replied, "I am. But you can call me by my birth name. Emily."

The young man said, "I am White Fox, son of Young Dragging Canoe. He has sent me to deliver these ponies to you."

Emily said, "Oh, well you must thank your father for me. I'm so happy that he was able to have them delivered so quickly."

White Fox then asked, "May we see the giant?"

"The giant?" asked Emily.

"Yes. The giant that pulled against four of my father's ponies."

Emily responded, "Well, sure! Come on over to the corral. We'll put the ponies in there, and you can see Pepper."

Emily led the young men to the corral, where they penned the Indian ponies with the rest of the stock. The horses were small compared to the mules and Emily and Daniel's other horses. Hoss stood fifteen hands, but these ponies were more like twelve or thirteen hands high. The first was a buckskin-colored mare with a black mane and tail. The second mare was solid white with pale blue eyes. The third was a pinto with brown spots. The final was an Appaloosa that was white except for brown specks on her rump. Four horses, all mares. Emily was ecstatic. She had four new mares to breed. She would be able to start a herd of horses that most breeders would envy.

The two young men jumped from their horses to the ground and walked to the corral, searching for the giant. Emily let out an ear-piercing whistle. Pepper and Rusty looked up from their grazing spot at the far end of the pasture. When they saw Emily, they both trotted over to her. White Fox and his companion backed away from the fence as the mules approached. The enormous size of the two mules was most intimidating. White Fox asked, "You have two giants?"

"Yes," said Emily. "They are called mules. This is Rusty, and this one is Pepper."

The young men joined Emily at the gate to examine her impressive animals closely. White Fox watched as Emily stroked the side of Pepper's face gently.

"Go ahead," she said. "You can touch them. They are very gentle."

The young men each reached up to touch one of the mules. Rusty snorted, startling the boys. They balked, holding their hands up in the air.

"He's just smelling you. He won't hurt you. He's just curious."

White Fox reached up again and finally found the nerve to touch Rusty on the face. The soft skin of Rusty's muzzle was comforting to touch. White Fox felt the warm air exiting Rusty's nostrils as he exhaled. As he became braver, he rubbed and caressed Rusty's face using both hands. He smiled as he petted the gentle giant.

"My father told me of this great animal, but I thought he was playing with me. I didn't believe an animal this size existed. He allowed me to deliver the ponies so I could see for myself. Thank you. Thank you for showing them to me."

Emily replied, "You're welcome. Come and visit whenever you want to see them again. How about some food. Can I fix you something to eat before you leave?"

"No, thank you. We must go. We have to meet my father on the trail. We are going home to Chickamauga."

Emily said, "Well, White Fox. Tell your father, thank you for me. And thank you for bringing the ponies to me. It was very nice to meet you."

The two young men mounted their ponies and galloped up the hill, leaving the Water Valley. Emily stood for a while, admiring her new stock.

CHAPTER 24

Daniel was tired from the arduous journey he and Susan had encountered. He found an empty tent to sleep in for the night. As he lay on his bedroll, he pulled out the diary and read the next entry.

March 14, 1780

The post arrived at Fort Nashborough today. I was surprised to see a letter to me from Timothy. I never expected to hear from him again since our last meeting. He said that he has gone east to fight in the revolution. He is serving under George Rogers Clark. He said he won't be back until the war has ended. He said I could have all of the traps if I wanted to continue trapping. I'm not sure if I want to anymore, but I need to do something to make money.

May 11, 1780

Many of the men have left Nashborough to fight in the war. I have managed to stay out of it. I'm sure many think ill of me in doing so, but I have stayed alive here in the frontier for nearly seven years, and I don't intend to lose my life in some war. I have found another way to serve the people of Tennessee. I am hunting and trapping. I furnish meat for the women who are unable to hunt for themselves. I trade the meat for items that I might need. I also

make items to trade, such as mittens, mufflers, and coats from the pelts that I trap. So far, things are going well.

May 16, 1780

The noon sun beat down like a drum on Gus's head as he walked through the open sage grass field leading to Mr. Robertson's farm. James Robertson was one of the founders of the fort and community, which was now called Nashborough. Gus was touring the area around the fort, meeting with families who might require his services as a trapper and hunter. Everyone in the community liked Gus. They recognized him as an honest soul. He had come to help them when the fort caught fire during its construction. They were grateful for his services as a provider while many men were away fighting for the revolution.

Robertson was not one of those men fighting for the cause. He was indeed for the cause but felt a more pressing obligation to provide leadership for the community, which Robertson and John Donelson had begun just five months earlier.

Donelson would be thirty-eight years old next month. He was tall and wiry in stature. Donelson was a capable hunter and trapper himself. Earlier in life, he had spent some time hunting and exploring the frontier with his friend and companion, Daniel Boone.

Gus liked talking to Robertson. He loved hearing his old stories of exploring the wilderness beside Boone. The only thing Gus had ever known about Daniel Boone was what he had seen on television as a kid. He was excited to talk with someone who had *actually* known the man and worked with him.

When Gus arrived, he found Robertson putting new shoes on his horses' hooves. Gus watched with interest as Robertson trimmed one of the horse's feet while supporting it between his knees. Robertson trimmed along the edge of the hoof with a pair of nippers, much like cutting someone's fingernails. Then, he rasped them down with a file to even out the edges. He used a hoof knife to clean out the dirt embedded inside the hoof, then trimmed the frog in the middle of the foot. Then, Donelson took a new metal shoe and sized it to fit the horse's hoof by bending it with a hammer over the end of an anvil. He would heat the horseshoe in a bed of fiery coals, then bang the metal into the correct shape and size. Donelson would then cool the shoe in a bucket of water and place it against the hoof to ensure it was the proper size and shape. Once satisfied, he nailed the shoe to the horse's hoof using small, squared-headed nails. Gus was fascinated by the whole process.

Just as Robertson had finished the last shoe, a rider came in from the east. It was Seth Akers. Akers and his wife had settled on a small farm east of Robertson's farm. He was a young man, not much older than Gus. His wife had died not long after they settled in the area. She was thrown from a horse while riding one day. Her head hit an outcropping of limestone, and the blow killed her instantly. Seth now struggled to farm alone.

Akers was breathless when he rode up to Robertson at a gallop. "Mr. Robertson, there's a British patrol heading this way. They hit my place about an hour ago while I was working in the field. They are stealing everything they can get their hands on."

Robertson replied, "Sounds like a conscription patrol. They'll take young men like yourself and force them into service. They'll also strip the farms of everything they can, to supply their troops. We've got to warn everyone."

Robertson turned to Gus and asked, "Gus, can you ride a horse?"

"Yes, sir. It's been a while since I've been on one, but I can ride."

Robertson continued, "Alright, take that Bay and ride north and west. Warn everyone that the British are moving toward us. Tell everyone to pack up supplies quickly and head to the fort. Seth, you ride south and west and do the same. I'll meet you at the fort as soon as I can get my family packed up and moving."

Gus and Seth rode out to fulfill Robertson's instructions. Gus knew all of the farms that surrounded the fort. There were nearly forty farms in the settlement. He had seen them all while trading his furs and services as a hunter. They all knew him and trusted him.

Robertson's farm would probably be the next one to be hit by the British if they continued to travel west along the trail. He had to pack up his things and his family quickly. They only took what they could pack on the backs of their horses or carry themselves. They concentrated on food and weapons. These would be things that the British would be looking for. Furniture and farm implements would be useless to them, so Robertson left them behind. The soldiers would most likely destroy them as they searched the premises, but Robertson could replace them.

Gus rode quickly through the hills and valleys that surround Fort Nashborough. He moved from farm to farm, announcing Robertson's instructions that everyone should run to the fort. When Gus arrived at Fort Nashborough, the sun quickly faded to the west. His horse was fatigued, and so was Gus. The fort was steadily filling with families and their supplies. John Donelson was there, instructing everyone where they should go. He was another of the founders of the Tennessee settlement that had arrived six months earlier.

Donelson was an older gentleman, sixty-two. The community respected him well. He was a master craftsman who worked with iron early on in life. But now, he was a public leader and politician in the new settlement.

His daughter, Rachel, would eventually marry the great General Andrew Jackson.

Donelson barked out orders as every new family arrived at the fort. He posted men along the fort's walls, concentrating mainly on the eastern wall. Women were also posted since some of their husbands were away fighting in the revolution. Many of the men who remained were only boys. It wasn't likely that the British would attack at night, but he had watchmen nevertheless. The men and women would sleep in shifts of four hours. They slept with their weapons at hand just in case the attack was to come during the night. Gus was exhausted from his long ride, so he slept during the first shift.

Sometime around two o'clock, Robertson roused Gus from a deep sleep. "Gus, it's your shift. I need you on the east wall."

Gus sleepily went to the wall and climbed up to take his post. There was a new moon that night, so it was very dark. Only the stars supplied any semblance of light. Gus stood at the wall and thought to himself. He had stayed here to avoid the war, and now it seemed it had come to him. He wasn't happy about it either.

The sun began to peek above the eastern hills around five o'clock. Gus searched the area in front of him for any movement. His senses were more intent now. He wiped his blurry eyes, trying to see more clearly. A fog bank had rolled in during the early hours, making it difficult to see. Gus cocked his ear toward the east suddenly when he thought he heard something in the distance. He looked around at his companions to see if anyone else had heard it. Everyone else seemed oblivious to any noise. Then, he heard it again. It was a low murmur. Someone in the distance was talking to someone else.

Gus turned back to look for Robertson. He found him. Twenty yards in the distance, he was standing on the ground, conversing with Donelson.

Gus tried to get their attention by waving his hand. It was no use. They ignored his efforts. Gus then looked around to find something he could throw toward them to gain their attention. He didn't want to yell out. He thought it better to keep quiet so the soldiers would think they had still not been discovered. Gus took out a mini-ball from his ammo pouch and threw it at Robertson. The lead shot hit Robertson in the right shoulder. He turned to see who or what had hit him. He had a look of disdain on his face. When he saw Gus waving to him, he understood. Robertson moved into a position next to Gus. Gus pointed into the fog and whispered, "I heard men talking out there. It might be scouts."

Robertson nodded understandingly, then moved down the line, letting every post know to be on alert. Gus turned his attention back to the fog and waited.

One hundred yards away, two British scouts moved through the fog together. They could barely see one another even though they were only twenty paces away. They spoke to each other in low tones as they blindly moved forward. They had no idea what lay on the other side of the fog. The first scout said to the other, "Hey, I think I see something up ahead."

"What is it?" the other man asked.

"I'm not sure. Let's get closer."

Gus watched as the two figures wearing red coats emerged from the fog. The man posted next to Gus raised his rifle and aimed. A shot exploded from the gun, sending smoke billowing in the air. Gus watched as the first scout was struck by the speeding projectile and then fell to the ground dead. The second scout, momentarily shocked at seeing a fortress standing before him, turned to run away. Another shot rang out, and the scout was struck in the back. Gus was stunned as he saw the two men die. He flashed back to the day when his friend Robbie had been killed. He closed his eyes and breathed in deeply, trying to overcome the anxiety building up within him. This situation went against everything his family stood for. They were hippies. Make love, not war. Gus had struggled since he came to this world, killing animals to survive. Now, he was being asked to kill men.

Then, it happened. One hundred or more red coats emerged from the fog. They fired their weapons simultaneously toward the fort. A bullet struck the man standing next to Gus and killed him. Gus panicked at the sight of the man having his brains blown out of the back of his head. Then, out of nowhere, Gus thought, "*It's you or them. It's time to man up.*"

While the soldiers were reloading their weapons, the settlers took the opportunity to fire against them. Twenty rifles volleyed lead shot at the red coats. Gus struck a man in the shoulder and knocked him down. "Not good enough," he said to himself.

He reloaded and retook aim. This time, he took a deep breath and slowly let it out as he aimed, just as Timothy had taught him. Gus said to himself, "It's just like shooting varmints."

His shot was true. He hit a man in the chest just as the soldier raised his rifle to aim. The red coat fell to the ground and died. The British pressed forward. Gus thought it absurd yet uncommonly brave for these men to attack against their fortress in this manner. They had no cover except the fog, yet they continued to move toward the fort.

Several red coats tried to ignite the fort by tossing torches at its base or over the walls, hoping to hit a keg of black powder. They never made it close enough to set fire to anything except themselves as they fell to the ground after being shot by the settlers. The skirmish lasted no more than thirty minutes. Gunsmoke and fog filled the air around the fort as the gunshots subsided.

It was two hours later before the fog lifted. The settlers didn't dare leave their fortress until they had a clear view of what lay ahead. Four scouts were sent out to track the British to verify whether they had retreated from the battleground or if they were somewhere hiding in ambush. They determined that the red coats had fled. Two acres on the east side of the fort were riddled with red coats soaked in blood. A few were still alive when the scouts relieved them of their pain by shooting them in the head. Forty-three British bodies lay dead in the field. Forty-seven graves would need to be dug. Four of the settlers had been killed as well.

May 17, 1780

Our fort was attacked by British soldiers yesterday. Four of our brave men were killed in the battle. Many others were wounded. We killed forty-three of them before they retreated. I had hoped to evade the war by staying here at the fort

rather than joining the ranks of colonial soldiers. I was wrong about that. I was not wrong about the war, however. I hope I never have to fire my rifle at another man as long as I live.

CHAPTER 25

June 20, 1819

Daniel retired to one of the tents at the Gordon encampment for the night. He and Susan would stay for the night, then leave in the morning to return to the Water Valley. Before bedding down for the night, he pulled out the diary and read for a while.

April 4, 1799

I can't believe what I witnessed today. A man named Andrew Pierce was caught stealing a horse. It seems horse thieves are the worst kind of thieves around here. He was sentenced to stand chained to the public pillory outside the courthouse for one hour. He was then given thirty-nine lashes with a whip. They then cut off both of his ears and branded his cheeks. One side with an H and the other with a T. It was a gruesome sight.

April 3, 1799

It was a morning much like any other. The sun rose, and the wind was cool. Gus tied his horse to a hitching rail outside the post office and entered the building to begin his work day. He found John Gordon inside. Gordon was already sorting mail that came in from North Carolina. Some of the mail was for the residents of Nashville and the surrounding areas. The rest would be sent down the line through the Natchez Trail.

Gus joined John in sorting the remaining mail and parcels that Gus would distribute on the post-ride. Citizens within Nashville would pick up their mail from the post office.

Gus carried mail on four different routes. It took him a full day to carry the mail from farm to farm. Each day, Gus would ride a twenty-mile area to deliver the post. People of the community always looked forward to the arrival of the post rider. He carried important news, letters from back east, or parcels that the farmers had ordered from mail-order catalogs. Everyone liked Gus. He was friendly, dependable, and trustworthy.

Close by, another young man was wandering around town. Andrew Pierce had recently traveled from Raleigh, North Carolina, with a group of families moving west. No one seemed to know much about him, not even the families he had traveled with. He kept to himself most of the time. That's just the way he liked it.

Andrew was eighteen years old. He had been on his own since the age of fourteen. His mother died at his birth from complications. His father was killed by the Cherokee while hunting on their lands. Andrew was a quiet yet angry young man. He felt as if life had dealt him a poor hand. He never caught a break. He had hoped things would change for him in Nashville. Maybe he could find work and make a life for himself here.

It was not to be, however. No one would hire him, and nobody was willing to give him a chance. Everyone looked upon him with disdain and suspicion. He was forced to walk the streets begging or looking for food scraps and sleeping wherever he could find a spot out of the weather.

After months of living on the streets, Andrew finally gave up. He needed to get away. He decided to travel west toward the Mississippi River and, if necessary, hop on a boat toward New Orleans. He was determined not to walk, however.

The next morning, Andrew woke up early and strode through the streets of Nashville, searching for an easy target. He found that target in the person of Gus Childers. He saw Gus ride up to the post office early and saw him tie up his horse outside. Andrew walked stealthily toward the post office, scanning his surroundings. When satisfied that no one was looking, Andrew untied the mare and swung himself into the saddle. He kicked the horse in the side, turned her west, and rode out of town.

After Gus and John finished sorting the mail that Gus would be delivering for the day, Gus placed the mail in saddlebags and proceeded to the door to mount up and begin his route. When he opened the door and walked outside, he saw that the mare was no longer tied to the hitching rail where he had left her. He looked left and right, hoping she was wandering down the street somewhere. Then he looked at the ground in front of the rail and observed that she had apparently left in a hurry, going west.

Gus ran back inside to tell John. "My horse is missing!"

John responded, "Did she wander off?"

"No!" replied Gus. "Her tracks show she took off at a gallop heading west."

John said, "We better get the sheriff."

Gus ran across the street to the courthouse where the local sheriff's office was situated. The office was on the east end of the courthouse, and the jail was standing directly behind. With a breathless voice, Gus pushed the door open and yelled, "My horse has been stolen, Sheriff!"

Sheriff Joshua Taylor was a middle-aged man of about forty. He was well-groomed and well-dressed. He wore a three-cornered hat and black leather boots. "Hold on there, young man. What's this here, you say?"

Gus replied, "I'm Gus Childers. I am the post rider. I left my horse tied up outside the post office this morning while I sorted the mail for today's route. When I went outside to start my run, my horse was gone. The tracks show she took off at a gallop heading west."

The sheriff asked, "Are you a tracker?"

Gus said, "Yes sir. I used to track and hunt this area many years before Nashville was built."

Taylor then asked, "Well what makes you so sure that your horse was stolen and didn't just take off on its own?"

Gus replied, "The tracks indicate she had a rider. They cut into the ground more deeply than if she were without a rider."

Taylor turned to one of his deputies, Charles Redman, and told him, "Charlie, go saddle up three horses and meet us outside."

Charlie did as he was instructed. Gus followed the sheriff outside so they could inspect the tracks together. Gus showed Taylor the tracks in front of the post office. John came outside to include himself in the conversation. "You see here, sheriff? That's her tracks. They head off that way."

Taylor said, "I'll have to take your word for it, young man. I'm not a tracker myself. I couldn't tell a horse track from a cow track."

Charlie rode up on his horse with two other horses in tow. Taylor told Gus, "You'll need to ride with us so you can track whoever it is that stole your horse. Gus looked back to John to get his approval. John nodded to Gus, letting him know it was alright.

The three men rode west out of town following the trail the horse thief had cut. About five miles out of town, Gus slowed to a walk. "Look, here! He's slowed up here. He's walking the horse now. We can probably catch up to him if we keep a canter."

Sheriff Taylor nodded, and they all cantered their horses, continuing west on the trail. They rode for about an hour when they came to a junction. The trail they had been following was a small path leading west deeper into the frontier. If they turned left, they would find themselves on the Natchez Trail. They pulled up their mounts momentarily to allow Gus to check the tracks.

"Can you tell which direction he went?" asked the sheriff.

Gus answered, "Yeah, he turned off to the left on this larger trail."

Taylor said, "That's the Natchez Road. He's headed south, now."

They turned their horses south and continued to canter. An hour later, they spotted a rider in the distance. It was Andrew Pierce. He turned and looked behind. When he spotted three riders approaching him, he kicked the mare into a gallop. The Duck River was just ahead. If he could cross, he might be able to outrun them. He spotted a clearing next to the river where an apparent crossing existed. He turned the mare toward the river and kicked her again. The mare saw the rushing waters of the Duck and balked to a halt, sending Andrew flying over her head into the river.

Andrew screamed, "Help! I can't swim!"

Gus quickly jumped from his horse and dove into the river to rescue the thief. The water quickly carried the two of them downstream for about one hundred feet before the sheriff and deputy were able to ride downriver to lend aid. Gus reached Andrew and held him out of the water while he searched for an exit. A fallen tree with its branches hanging out over the water was his best chance. He carefully sited his target and timed his leap just in time to catch one of the branches. He held the branch in one hand with Andrew in the other.

Deputy Redman climbed the fallen tree to help Gus lift the thief out of the water. Andrew coughed and vomited up water that he had unintentionally swallowed. Once everyone managed to get their breathing sorted out, they mounted back up and rode toward Nashville. They rode much slower, so it took them almost twice as long to return. They rode into Nashville around two o'clock and stopped in front of the courthouse.

Taylor told Gus, "We'll need you to come into the courthouse to testify if the judge deems it necessary."

Gus nodded and followed them in.

The Honorable Allistair Robinson was the judge presiding over the court. He was a man of ill-temper, old, grey, and wrinkled. No one had ever seen him smile.

The four men entered the back of the courtroom and stood quietly while the judge finished with another case. "Thomas Jennings, this court finds you guilty of being drunk and disorderly in a public place. I sentence you to five days in jail and restitution for any damages caused."

The judge banged his gavel, signifying that the case was over. The bailiff took Jennings into custody and escorted him to the jail.

The judge looked up, spotted Sheriff Taylor in the back of the courtroom, and beckoned him forward. Taylor moved forward, dragging Pierce with him. They stood together in front of the judge and waited.

The judge spoke, "What is the name of the accursed?"

Taylor waited for Pierce to speak. When he didn't speak, Taylor nudged Pierce with his elbow, prodding him to speak. "Uh, Andrew Pierce, sir."

"Sheriff what is this man accused of?"

"He's a horse thief, Your Honor."

The judge stared with wide eyes at the young man, and Gus thought he had almost seen the judge's lips curl up at the end. "Well, Mr. Pierce, what do you have to say for yourself?"

"Nothing, sir. I did it. I stole a horse. I just wanted to get out of here."

Judge Robinson asked, "Do you not find our community delightful? Is there something wrong with Nashville? What would make you so desperate to steal another man's horse?"

"I got here over a month ago. I've been trying to find work, but nobody will hire me. I've been starving and I just couldn't take it anymore, so I took the first horse I could find and left."

The judge cleared his throat and said, "Well then, Andrew Pierce, you have been found guilty by this court of horse thievery. Your sentencing will be carried out immediately and is as follows. You will stand in public humiliation between the pillars outside this courthouse for one hour. After which, you will receive thirty-nine lashes by our sheriff or one of his deputies. You then will have your ears docked and then be branded as a horse thief. Do you have any questions?"

"No sir."

"Sheriff, carry out the sentence, please."

Sheriff Taylor took Pierce by the arm and escorted him out of the courtroom. Gus and the deputy followed. Gus was shocked by what he had just heard. He had no idea that stealing a horse called for such barbaric punishment.

Pierce was taken outside and chained between the two pillars in front of the courthouse. Observers who had witnessed the proceedings in the courtroom dashed outside and started spreading the news to everyone in town. People came from everywhere to witness and partake in the public humiliation of the young man. Many threw rocks or rotten produce at him as he stood between the pillars, unable to dodge the projectiles.

A blacksmith was called to make a fire for the final part of the punishment. He set up his gear at the far end of the courthouse steps. He used a set of bellows to warm the coals of the fire until they were glowing red with heat. Two small branding irons were placed in the fire. Each had a letter at the end. One had an "H" while the other had a "T".

After an hour, Pierce had his shirt ripped from his body, exposing his bare torso. Deputy Redman was given the task of whipping Andrew. Redman stood behind Andrew while Andrew faced the mob. Gus watched from inside the post office with tears in his eyes as Pierce endured lash after lash. The crowd counted off each one. "*Twelve, thirteen, fourteen . . .*"

Andrew screamed out as each slash of the whip cut into his skin, exposing muscle. "*Twenty-eight ... twenty-nine ... thirty . . .*"

Blood flowed from the young thief's body, dropping onto the steps of the courthouse. Andrew's head dropped as his strength left his body. "*Thirty-seven ... thirty-eight ... thirty-nine!*"

Andrew was barely standing as the sheriff walked up to him with a knife in his hand. With little concern or emotion, Taylor grabbed Andrew's left ear and sliced it off with the knife. He dropped the severed ear to the ground, then grabbed Andrew's right ear and sliced it off as well. Andrew wailed as tears flowed down his cheeks. "No more! Please! No more!" he cried out.

Taylor then nodded to the blacksmith, who walked over holding the two branding irons. Each of the deputies held Andrew while the blacksmith presented the first iron to the sheriff. The blacksmith stepped behind Andrew and grabbed a handful of his hair, turning Andrew's head to expose his right cheek to the sheriff. Taylor pressed the iron into Andrew's right cheek and held it there for several seconds. When he pulled it away, what once was a smooth young cheek was now red and charred. A two-inch tall "H" had been burned into Andrew's skin. The blacksmith then handed Taylor the other iron and exposed Andrew's left cheek so that the procedure could be repeated. Taylor branded him with a "T". The pain was so unbearable that Andrew passed out and was left hanging between the pillars.

Gus couldn't believe his eyes. He sobbed as he watched the sheriff and his men unchain Andrew's unconscious body from the pillars. The crowd continued to yell and cheer as the young man was dragged away.

Gus turned away from the window and looked John in the eyes while he continued to weep.

Chapter 26

June 21, 2018

As Gus lay on the ground, he saw the gateway close. The sun was gone. He wasn't sure where or when he might be. He could only hope, for now, that he had made it to 2018. He saw no point in trying to find his way to the Gordon House in the dark. So, he looked for a suitable place to spread out his blanket for the night. He moved away from where Ittola Chuka had opened for fear that he might be back in 1818. He knew that if he had somehow come back to 1818, he would most likely have to deal with Ilbuk Losa, the Black Hand.

Gus didn't sleep well that night. His mind raced with thoughts about his situation. Would he finally get to see his parents after forty-six years? Would they still be alive? The anticipation was killing him. He tried not to think about it anymore. But, his mind would eventually turn back to the same thoughts repeatedly.

When dawn finally approached, Gus praised the sun for eventually rising. He gathered up his belongings and headed toward what he hoped would be the Gordon House. Gus decided to check his surroundings. He wanted to be able to find this place again. There was a Dogwood tree just five feet from where the opening had occurred the day before. He rummaged through his things, looking for something he could use as a marker. All he could find that might be used was his old tie-dyed T-shirt. He climbed the tree as far up as he could and tied the shirt to one of the upper branches. He hoped that anyone who happened by here wouldn't be curious enough to climb the tree if they happened to see the shirt. Then, he climbed back down.

Emily had told him that a rest stop now stood at the Gordon exhibit. There were restrooms, and he should be able to flag someone down eventually to borrow their cell phone to call for help. *"A bathroom! Oh, I can't wait to sit on an actual toilet again,"* he said to himself. *"And real toilet paper."*

He had used an outhouse or the outdoors for so long now that it didn't seem possible to use a proper facility finally. No more leaves or corn husks. He couldn't wait.

He walked south and west for about forty-five minutes, fighting briars and vines through the forest. He finally could hear the river up ahead in the distance. His heart began to beat faster with anticipation. He moved upstream when he reached the river, searching for something familiar. The terrain was quite different from his days as a teenager when he and Robbie explored this area. It was different from what he had lived in as an adult. He became nervous that he might not be in the right place or time after all.

Then, his heart sank as he spotted a familiar sight up ahead. A ferry. His ferry. Only it was different. The barge was newer than the one he and Tom had operated together. The platform wasn't made of logs but of lumber. The floor of the barge was flat. Someone must have updated it.

Gus approached the ferry to get a closer look. He saw two individuals working around the barge, keeping it maintained. Gus could see that there was an older black man who looked like he could barely walk as he got closer. There was also a black boy that looked about ten years old. The man looked slightly startled when Gus came out of the brush.

Gus asked the man, "Excuse me, is this the Gordon Ferry?"

The man looked puzzled but responded, "Naw, suh. This here's da Kennedy Ferry."

Gus thought for a moment. The slave he met yesterday, or whenever it was, told him that Travis Kennedy was the new owner of what was once the Gordon Place. Then Gus asked, "Travis Kennedy?"

"Naw, suh. Don't know, no Travis Kennedy. This here b'longs ta Masta Will Kennedy."

Then Gus asked, "Is there a brick house close by? It used to belong to Captain John Gordon."

The man answered, "Well, let's see. There used to be a brick house up yonder 'bout half a mile. But, it's been knocked over a bit. Got messed up durin' da war."

"Which war?" asked Gus.

"The war twixt da north and da south."

Gus asked, "You mean the Civil War? The one back in the 1860s?"

The old man replied, "Dat sounds 'bout right."

"What year is it now?"

"Well, suh. It's uh . . ."

The young boy spoke for the first time, "It's 2018, suh!"

Gus's jaw dropped. How could it be? Something had gone wrong. How could he be at the right time, but things were so wrong? It was as if everything was stuck in the late 1800s.

Gus looked around for help. There was none. He thought to himself, "How can this be happening again? I should have just stayed with Daniel. Now I'm stuck here for six months."

Gus then asked, "Is there a town nearby?"

The old man said, "'Bout twenty mile to the east. Ever thang round here b'long to Masta Will. Day say he own 'bout fifteen thousand acres."

Gus asked, "What's the name of the town?"

"Columbia," said the old man.

Then Gus asked, "Is this the Duck River?"

"Yeah, suh."

Gus thought for a moment. He could float down the Duck River all the way to Columbia.

"Mista! Just so's you knows, Masta Will don't like no strangers. He don't like no trespassers neither. Don't let him sees you round here none. He shoot you dead."

Gus asked, "Where does he live?"

"He stay in the valley east of here bout four hours ride by hoss."

Gus clarified, "The Water Valley?"

"Yeah, suh."

Gus reached into a poke that was tied to his belt and pulled out a five-dollar gold piece. He handed it to the old man and said, "You never saw me. Alright?"

The man looked at the gold piece and smiled. He had only four teeth, but Gus could see them all. "No, suh. We ain't see nobodies."

Gus turned away and headed back the way he came. He crept, searching for something he could use as transportation down the river. Gus knew it would be unlikely that he would happen upon a canoe. Besides, a boat would be too conspicuous if he were going to pass by Kennedy's home without being noticed.

He moved around a bend in the river and finally spotted what he was searching for. A fallen tree lay at the river's edge, which was relatively large, about twenty-four inches in diameter. It was only about twelve feet long. There were a few branches, but they weren't too large. He took his tomahawk out from his belt and hacked at the limbs until he was able to remove them. He left a couple of the branches about six inches long so he would have handholds. He then rolled the log into the edge of the river.

Before pushing it into the water, he collected all of his gear. He then waded into the water and pulled the log into the water with him. He knew that the Water Valley would lie to the left side of the river as he floated by, so he kept the log between him and the left bank.

The water was reasonably swift as it swept Gus downstream. He initially struggled to find his balance because the log kept turning over in the water as the current pushed it downstream. Eventually, he found the sweet spot that allowed him to coast along with the log without much effort.

Gus kept his eyes on both banks of the river. He wanted to avoid being seen by anyone at this point. He didn't know anyone, and therefore, there was no one he could trust. The Duck was deeper and broader than he had remembered it. Undoubtedly, two hundred years of erosion had caused the river to grow. The summer rains had filled it so that the current was swift.

Tall trees lined the banks of the river. Oaks, Pines, and Cedars towered over him as he floated along. He could hear mockingbirds singing their songs, even over the loud rush of the muddy waters. After about an hour, the trees became more sparse on the left bank. Gus suspected that he was approaching Water Valley.

He carefully peeked over the top of the log as he came closer. He regularly checked the right bank as well. Gus noticed that the log seemed to be drifting toward the left bank. He kicked with his feet against the current, struggling to keep the log from going aground. He then noticed two people up ahead. A man and a young boy were standing next to the river bank. The boy had a fishing pole with the line bobbing up and down in the water.

The youngster noticed Gus's log as it approached. "Papa, look at that log floating in the river!"

"Yes!" said the boy's father. "Isn't that something."

Gus ducked his head to conceal himself from the two onlookers. He debated whether or not he should duck under the water. He tried not to kick against the current while passing them, but the log was steering too close to suit Gus. He stretched out his legs to give a good kick but found shallow water. Instead of kicking, he walked along next to the log, dragging it away from the bank. As he floated past the two, he attempted to turn the tree trunk so that he would be concealed from them as he drifted away.

As Gus continued downriver, he saw a large plantation-style home erected in the valley. At the back of the house was an expansive flower garden with a gazebo sitting in the center of it. Off in the distance was a large barn with a gambrel-style roof. Many slaves could be seen moving about on the property. Gus still pondered how things could have gotten so messed up. How did the South win its independence from the federal government of the United States? He wished Daniel were there so he could ask him about it.

The ride down the river was reasonably smooth and without incidence once he cleared the Water Valley. An hour later, he arrived in Columbia. He decided to exit the river before he made it into town. He would find a place to hide while his clothes could dry.

Gus recalled that the Duck River flowed just north of Columbia, so once his clothes were dry, he began walking south toward town. After walking for thirty minutes, he found a road. Gus followed the path that led into the city. He realized that he hadn't eaten in almost two days. Gus hoped that he could trade for some food and maybe find work. He would need a place to stay for the next six months until he could trek back through Ittola Chuka.

He came upon a cemetery on the left side of the road as he neared the town. He could see several buildings about a quarter of a mile down the road. He found stores, hotels, a bank, and a livery stable just inside the town. Gus decided to check out the livery. It was a large barn built from cedar boards. There was a loft that was half full of hay. Several stalls in the barn were on either side of an alley going down the middle of the barn.

Gus entered the barn and called out, "Hello?'

A man, whom Gus thought was about forty years old, came out from one of the stalls and said, "Yes. Can I help you?"

Gus replied, "Well, sir, my name is Gus. Gus Childers. I just got into town, and I wondered if you might know of someone in town who might be looking to hire some help."

The man looked at Gus and asked, "What kind of work? What can you do?"

Gus replied, "Well, I've done a lot in my lifetime. I ran a ferry for several years up on the Natchez Trail. I've done some farming. I was a post rider in my younger days. I'm a good hunter and trapper, and I'm pretty good at making mittens and other clothes out of furs."

"Do you know anything about horses?"

Gus said, "Oh, yes, sir. I've been around horses most of my life."

The man said, "Well, my wife has been after me to hire someone to help out here. I can't pay much. But there's a room with a bed over there in the corner. You can stay there as part of your pay. You can have your meals with me and my wife if you like."

Gus smiled and said, "Thank you, sir. That sounds very nice." Suddenly, Gus's stomach began rumbling.

The man said, "My name is Randall Autry. My wife is Barbara. It's nearly supper time now, so come on with me, and we'll get you fed. After supper, I'll show you to your bunk, and we'll talk about your duties."

Gus said, "Thanks, Mr. Autry. I surely appreciate your kindness."

"Just call me Randall."

Chapter 27

December 20, 2018

A winter cold front moved into middle Tennessee, bringing one of the worst ice and snowstorms the area had ever seen. Fourteen inches of snow covered the town of Columbia, and temperatures dipped below zero for the first time in over fifty years. No one moved about the city; everyone stayed shut up in their homes.

Gus was shut in as well. For the first time in forty years, he was sick. He wasn't sure if it was the flu or just a bad cold, but he felt horrible. He was disheartened. He knew that tomorrow was the day he should go through Ittola Chuka to return to Daniel. There wasn't much hope of that now. Even if he weren't sick, there wasn't much of a chance of his being able to get to Ittola Chuka in the blizzard that had set upon the area.

For six months, Gus had dreamed and planned about his trip back through the Shimmering. He had saved every penny Randall had paid him except for buying new clothes. He planned to save up enough money to purchase a canoe or a small boat so he could travel back up the Duck when the time came.

He hadn't made that purchase yet, which might be a while. He could barely stand because of his fever. Mrs. Autry had brought him soup and other food several times over the past few days. While most employers would not be as understanding, Randall handled most of Gus's chores. He was a kind person. He recognized what a good hand Gus was too.

So, for now, Gus tried to concentrate on getting healthy. He would have another opportunity in another six months.

June 20, 2019

Gus had been thinking about his return for almost a year. He had tried to plan out everything just right but didn't want to say anything to Randall about his leaving. Gus knew it was inconsiderate to just up and go without notice. But Gus needed to keep the element of secrecy intact. If things didn't work out for some reason, he could come back here and continue his job. He would make up an excuse about getting lost or something.

Gus had met a trapper earlier in the year and made a deal with him to purchase a canoe. It was a little longer than Gus had hoped for, but he was sure he could handle it by himself. Gus had hidden the canoe down by the river two days ago. He checked on it last night to make sure it had not been stolen. It was still there.

After supper, Gus excused himself from the Autrys and returned to the barn as usual. Dusk wouldn't arrive until after eight-thirty, so he anxiously waited in his bunk. Gus tried to sleep for a while. He finally drifted off to sleep but woke suddenly around midnight.

Gus sneaked out of the barn and headed for the Duck, where his canoe awaited him. He threw his sparse belongings into the vessel and shoved off. The trip would be more complicated than riding a log down the river with the current. He had to paddle against the river's current. He struggled at first to keep the canoe moving straight. After a while, he got the hang of it and could move up the river with some effort.

Two hours later, Gus was exhausted from paddling. He spotted the valley where Will Kennedy's home lay. Gus decided to lay up on the bank for a while to rest. He chose the bank on his right, which was closest to the valley. Gus thought concealment would be more natural there. He reached into his bag, pulled some jerky, and chewed on it. He felt he needed some extra energy to complete the trip upriver.

After a thirty-minute rest, he shoved off again and paddled upstream. He continuously checked the valley for any movement. He still had the cover of darkness for another two hours, but he thought someone moving around in the valley might spot him.

After another hour of paddling, he saw the ferry lying up ahead. The ferry was the point at which he could measure his bearing. He stopped and turned the canoe so he could float back downriver. He needed to find the point along the river where he had arrived the year before. He couldn't remember exactly where he had initially found the river, so he decided to float for about half a mile. He then pulled up on the bank. He pulled the canoe up out of the water and concealed it with fallen tree branches. He hoped he would not need it again, but it would be here if he needed to escape quickly.

Satisfied that the canoe was well hidden, he began his trek into the forest to find his destination. He crept through the brush. He had no idea if anyone might be around that could spot him. He took no chances. Every time he heard an unfamiliar sound, he froze. An hour later, he came to the edge of the forest. An open area lay in front of him. Beyond that, a wooded area lay in front of him about a quarter of a mile into the distance. The sun was rising. People began stirring around the area. He couldn't leave the shelter of the forest for fear of being spotted by someone.

Groups of slaves moved down the road that was situated between him and his target. Horses pulling wagons were driven down the road in front of him. People were continually going and coming toward what once was the Gordon House from the Water Valley Plantation. Gus had no choice. He would have to wait. Hopefully, he would find an opening before sunset. If not, he would be stuck here for another six months.

Gus began to grow sleepy. He had slept very little the night before, and it was now taking a toll on him. Gus decided it might be okay to find a spot to sleep. He picked out a large Oak tree and hid behind it on the opposite side of the road. He leaned against the tree and closed his eyes.

An hour later, Gus woke with a start. He looked around to see where he was. Then Gus remembered, so he crawled on his hands and knees through the brush toward the open field. He checked the sun. It was midday, by his estimation. Traffic through the open area had slowed substantially. He felt he could make it across to the woods on the other side of the clearing without being noticed.

He stood up, gathered himself, and walked casually across the open field. Gus tried to keep his composure and walk as if he belonged. But it was difficult because his heart was pounding, and his adrenaline was rushing. A group of slaves riding on a cart being pulled by a mule crossed the path behind him. He ignored them and kept walking.

Just as he reached the wooded area before him, two white men on horseback came riding up the trail. They noticed Gus and called out to him. "Hey! You There!"

Gus looked over his shoulder but kept on walking. The riders picked up their pace and continued to call out to Gus. "Hey! You! Stop!"

Gus quickly looked over his shoulder, then sprinted through the woods. He dodged trees, stumbled through dips in the terrain, and jumped over holes. Gus heard the horses coming after him. He kept his eyes forward and searched for his target. He looked for the Dogwood tree - the tree with his colorful shirt tied up on the top branch.

Gus began to doubt his sense of direction. He wondered if he had miscalculated the spot at which he should have exited the river. His head swiveled back and forth, searching for the tie-dyed flag at the top of the tree. He ran for a quarter of a mile until he finally spotted it. Up ahead and to the left. About three hundred yards in the distance.

A shot rang out close behind Gus. A bullet missed him but struck a low-lying branch just to his right. He ducked and changed direction but never stopped running. His legs were weary, and his lungs gasped for air—two hundred yards to go.

Gus dodged a fallen tree limb, then turned back to the right again. The ground sloped slightly upward. His thighs and calves were screaming. Gus kept moving. He heard another shot. This time, the bullet struck the ground right between his churning feet. Gus felt another burst of adrenaline enter his body. He picked up his stride and leaped over an outcropping of limestone. One hundred yards more.

Gus saw the shimmering light up ahead. The trees in front of him seemed to blur. A wave of light moved over the trees, making them look out of focus. Twenty yards. Another shot. This one was true. The bullet struck Gus in the back. He grunted, and his stride faltered, but he kept moving. "Help me, Lord!" he cried as he fell face-first through the Shimmering. He struggled to get to his feet. He looked around to see if Ilbuk Losa was coming. The Black Hand was sure to be nearby. When he managed to reach his feet, he took a sharp turn to the left and went around the gateway, heading back from where he had just come.

The two men following Gus balked at the sight of the shimmering waving in front of them. They spurred their horses through, continuing their pursuit of the trespasser. When they touched ground on the other side, they found themselves face to face with six painted men on horseback. They pulled up their horses to a stop, then tried to turn them back through the Shimmering. They were too late. Ilbuk Losa subdued the riders, knocking them off of their mounts.

Four of the braves dismounted and seized the two men. One brave took his tomahawk and split the first man's skull open. The second man screamed at the sight of his partner's brains being exposed. A second brave unsheathed his knife and put it to the man's throat. The brave grabbed a handful of the man's hair with his free hand while slicing through the man's neck. The cut was deep. Blood flowed freely down the man's shirt front. He choked and coughed while staring into the darkness of his mind. The brave let him loose, and he fell to his knees. Then he fell forward, face first, and landed on the body of his friend. The six members of Ilbuk Losa mounted their horses and rode away, leaving the bodies to be consumed by scavengers.

CHAPTER 28

June 21, 1819

Daniel slept late. The last few days had taken their toll on his body. Driving a carriage was quite different than riding in a saddle. His long legs were not used to being confined in such a small space. Exiting the tent, he found Susan having breakfast at the community table. He joined her at the table as one of the slave women brought him a plate and a cup of coffee. "Good morning," Daniel said to Susan. "Thanks!" he said to the woman.

He looked at Susan and asked, "Are you ready to go back to our valley?"

"I guess so," she responded. "I don't really know what I'll do, though. I don't know whether to go back to Virginia or find a place to settle around here. I thought about moving to Nashville, but I don't know what I would do once I got there."

Daniel said between bites of eggs and bacon, "Well, there's no hurry. You can stay with us for as long as you like. I know Emily is very fond of you. We've been needing to add a dogtrot to our cabin with an additional cabin. We can get started on that, so you'll have a proper room to stay in."

"I don't want you to go to all of that trouble for me. I'm fine for now in the wagon."

Daniel replied, "Well, whether you stay or not, I've got to build it. Emily needs a proper place for her medical practice. It will serve as an exam room and a hospital."

They finished eating their breakfast and then packed up the carriage. Tommy and Amy decided to ride along with them back to the Water Valley. Amy's sisters had already returned back to their homes in Nashville. Amy was ready to get back to her house, as well.

By the time they had left Dolly's, the sun was already beating down on them. The air was humid, making it difficult to breathe. They took it easy on the horses. They walked them at a leisurely pace. Daniel let his mind wander as he drove the Morgan down the trail. Susan opened up a fan and cooled herself as best she could. About an hour down the path, Daniel spotted something near the top of a Hickory tree. As they came closer, he realized what it was. Two bear cubs were taking a nap. Daniel pointed them out to the other travelers and said, "We best keep an eye out. The sow will be nearby."

They heard something moving around in the deep underbrush of the forest but never saw the sow. The mother was most likely feeding on blackberries, which seemed to be plentiful in the area. As long as they stayed on the trail, she would not bother them.

As they approached the area where the trail turned away from Ittola Chuka, Daniel spotted something lying on the trail. As they came closer, Daniel realized it wasn't just something but someone. He pulled up the horse about twenty feet shy of the body lying on the trail. He stepped down from the carriage, carrying his rifle with him. Tommy joined him. Whoever it was was injured. Daniel saw him take a deep breath. Then Daniel's heart began to race when he realized the man looked familiar. Even though his back was turned to Daniel, Daniel realized it was his old friend Gus.

Daniel raced to him and called out, "Gus!"

The old man groaned a bit. Daniel spotted what appeared to be a gunshot wound in his back. He knelt down and rolled him over. Daniel held

Gus in his arms while the two of them sat on the ground. He asked, "What happened, Gus? What are you doing back here?"

Gus looked up and asked, "Daniel? Is that you?"

"It's me, Gus. What happened to you? Who shot you?"

Gus coughed and replied, "Daniel, something went wrong. When I went through the Shimmering a year ago, it took me four hundred years into the future."

He continued between coughs, "I managed to go back through before the gateway disappeared. I finally made it to 2018. There's something wrong, though. When I was in 2218, nothing had changed. No new inventions like you told me about. Everything was just like it is in 1818, only worse. Slavery still exists. The south won their independence in the Civil War. When I made it back to 2018, it was the same. Daniel, something has changed the timeline."

Daniel asked, "How did you make it back to 2018 from 2218?"

Gus said, "It all depends on which direction you travel through the Shimmering."

Daniel asked, "Okay, we'll think about that later. Let's get you back to our farm so Emily can help you. Can you walk?"

Gus replied, "I'll try."

Daniel and Tommy lifted Gus to his feet and helped him back to the carriage. They helped him into the back seat, where he leaned over to rest himself across the bench as best he could. Daniel knew Gus had lost a lot of blood, so he pushed the Morgan to a steady trot. Susan's Morgan horse was an excellent trotter. He was swift and never broke his gate.

As they traveled down the trail, Daniel tried to encourage Gus to "Hold on!"

Gus would cough once in a while, letting Daniel know that he was at least still alive. Susan turned around often to check on Gus.

After thirty minutes or so of trotting, Daniel eased up on the Morgan to let him rest while walking. The horse was sweating profusely. After another thirty minutes of walking, Daniel picked up the pace once again. They continued this cycle until they finally made it back to the Water Valley. As they drove down the slope into the valley and crossed Beaver Branch, Daniel searched for Emily. He thought she would probably be at the cabin but wasn't sure.

Jake came running toward them from the horse corral. He barked with excitement at seeing Daniel's return. Daniel drove up to the cabin and stopped. He called out, "Emily!"

He jumped from the carriage, darted to the cabin door, and opened it. Emily wasn't there. He jumped from the cabin porch and turned toward the corral just as Emily appeared. Emily asked, "What are you shouting about?"

Daniel breathlessly said, "It's Gus! He's back, and he's injured!"

Emily rushed to the back of the carriage to find Gus lying over in the backseat. "What's wrong with him?"

Daniel replied, "He was shot in the back."

Emily opened up Gus's shirt and searched for any wounds. "I don't see an exit wound. The bullet must still be inside. Let's get him into the cabin."

Daniel and Tommy lifted Gus from the back of the carriage and carried him inside. Amy and Susan followed. Emily cleared the table and had them lower Gus onto it. She removed his shirt and jacket and said, "Help me turn him over so I can look at that wound."

Gus's breathing changed suddenly. It was more labored. He gasped for air. Emily quickly grabbed her stethoscope and listened to his heart and lungs. His heart was barely beating. She suspected from the sound of his breathing that one of his lungs had collapsed. "Daniel, go down to the river and cut me a Cattail reed. Quickly!"

Daniel did just as she instructed. He ran to the Duck and found an area where the Cattails were growing. Daniel took his knife out of its sheath and cut a length of Cattail about twelve inches long. He ran back to the cabin and showed Emily. "Is this long enough?"

"Yeah, too long. Make it about six inches and cut off the Cattail. I just need the reed. Make sure it's clear. Blow through it."

Daniel did as she said. He cut the reed to about six inches, then blew through the reed. "It's clear," he said.

Emily was turning Gus's body over to his back again with the help of Tommy when she said, "Okay, now sharpen one end of the reed to a point."

Emily cleaned Gus's chest with an iodine solution while Daniel sharpened the reed and handed it to her. Emily felt Gus's ribs and found the right spot to insert the reed. When she found what she was looking for, she used a scalpel to cut a slit, then placed the reed there. She then pushed the reed into Gus's body. Daniel and Tommy both winced at the sight of Emily pushing the reed into Gus's lung, but it worked. Gus began to breathe more easily.

Daniel asked, "Is he going to be okay?

Emily said, "He breathing better, but he's not out of the woods yet. He's still got a bullet in him. If that bullet went into his lungs, he's not likely to make it. I just don't have the knowledge or the equipment for that kind of surgery. He's lost a lot of blood too. All we can do is keep him as comfortable as possible."

Gus reached up and grabbed Daniel's arm. Daniel leaned over to Gus's face so he could hear him. Gus whispered because of his lack of strength, "They shot me."

"Who shot you, Gus?" asked Daniel.

The people who owned this valley in 2018. They own everything. Even the Gordon Place. They don't like strangers. I had to cross through to get to the Shimmering. They chased me and shot me. You got to . . ."

Gus released Daniel's arm, then closed his eyes and breathed his last breath. Tears welled up in Daniel's eyes. He pulled up a chair and sat next to Gus's lifeless body as it lay on the table. He reached out and held Gus's hand. Emily motioned to Tommy, Amy, and Susan. They all followed Emily outside to leave Daniel alone with his friend.

After a long while, Daniel composed himself and met the others outside on the porch. Tommy and Amy were just returning from the corral where they had unhitched the Morgan and unsaddled their horses. Emily embraced Daniel and said," I'm sorry. I know you and Gus had become very close."

Daniel smiled quickly and fought back the tears he felt might flow at any minute.

As Tommy and Amy rounded the corner of the cabin, Tommy said, "I seen you got some new horses out there."

Emily said, "Yeah, Young Dragging Canoe's son White Fox delivered them two days ago. He was very excited to see my two gentle giants."

Amy said, "Well, they sure are pretty. I especially like the look of that Appaloosa."

Emily replied, "Yeah, she's a beauty, alright. We've got four new mares now. With my Bay mare and Amy's mare, Hoss is going to be a happy stallion."

They all laughed. Even Daniel managed to smile at Emily's comment.

It was just before dusk when Tommy and Daniel had finished digging a grave for Gus. They laid him to rest in a spot just below the hill that led to the bluff on the far side of the valley. There was a large Oak tree there that would cover him for eternity. They all gathered to say one last goodbye to their old friend. Only Daniel knew the struggles that Gus had endured in his life. The hardships that he suffered trying to survive in a world so wild and untamed at such a tender age. Daniel held the diary as they gathered around the grave to honor Gus. Daniel said, "I thought I would read the last entry in Gus's diary to you rather than reading scripture."

He opened up the diary to the last page and read,

June 20, 1818

This will be my last entry. Daniel and I will be going home tomorrow. At least that is the plan. We still don't know for sure if it will work or not. It is just a theory that Daniel has. I told him that Robbie and I came through on June 21, 1973. He came through on December 21, 2017. So his theory is that the Shimmering only opens on the summer and winter solstice. We will test it out tomorrow. Cross your fingers. I haven't seen my home in such a long time. I can't wait to get there.

THE DIARY OF GUS CHILDERS

My name is August Moon Earthchild. I found this book by a river bed inside a leather bag. I don't know who it belonged to. I will use it to give an account of my time in this new world I have entered. I have tried to keep a count of the days that I have been here. I calculate it to be 22 days. If my count is correct, then today should be July 13th. I don't know how I got here. All I know is, I must have gone through a time portal of some sort. I don't know what year it is.

The only people I have seen are the ones who killed my friend Robbie. They were dressed as Indians. I found another group riding down the river in canoes the next day. I pray that they do not see me. I have spent most of my time along the river. I think it is the Duck unless I have been transported to a completely different world. I've been

surviving so far on berries and nuts. I retrieved the spear that was used to kill Robbie, but I have been unable to kill any wild game yet. If I don't figure out how to catch game soon, I will starve this winter. I hope to find civilization at some point, but for now, I will just try to stay alive.

A. E.

P.S. I wish I could awaken from this nightmare. I want to go home!

Day 30

I managed to spear a fish today in the river. I didn't have any matches, and I have been unable to start a fire. I'm not sure it would be a good idea anyway. The men who killed Robbie might see the smoke and come looking for me. So, I ate the fish raw. I also found some grub worms at the base of an old fallen tree. It's amazing what you can eat when you are starving.

Day 36

It rained really hard last night. I found a bluff to hide under on the river bank, but then the water began to rise, so I had to abandon it to look for another place out of the rain. I found a large fallen tree that helped a little, but I woke up this morning, soaking wet.

Day 44

If my calculations are correct, today is August 4th. Happy birthday to me. I'm now 17 years old.

Day 71

I've got to find someone. I'm starting to go a little bonkers. I find myself talking to the birds and insects because I'm so lonesome. Every few days, I see Indians floating up or down the river in canoes. I hide every time they pass. I can't find any more berries. I've picked them all, I guess. I've decided to move upriver to explore a bit. Maybe I can find someone to talk to.

Day 80

Things are really getting rough now. I haven't eaten in three days except for some leaves that smelled like mint. They tasted awful. Very bitter. There aren't any fish in this part of the river. At least, not close enough to the bank where I can spear them. I'll keep moving upstream tomorrow if I can find the strength.

October 2, 1773

I now know the date and the place that I now abide in. After spending much of the time by the river, trying to survive, I have developed enough skill with the spear to at least catch fish from time to time. The fish and the

blackberries and blueberries that I have been able to gather, have kept me alive.

Thirty-two days ago, I decided to leave my little camp at the river, which I now know to be the Duck River, and headed north and east. I stayed as close to the creeks and rivers as possible, following them upstream. Two days ago, I came across a trapper who was setting traps along the bank of what he told me was the Cumberland River. His name is Jasques-Timothee' Boucher de Montbrun. He said I could call him Timothy.

He has a camp set up in a cave that sits on a bluff right above the river. He said I could work for him and he gave me some warmer clothes to wear. Tomorrow, he said we will go to the salt lick to hunt for some wild game so he can harvest their hides.

He has been accommodating, but he is also a man of ill-temper when things don't go as he wishes. I am just happy to have someone to talk to again. I miss my family.

November 6, 1773

Timothy has been teaching me to shoot. He has given me one of his rifles. I had never even seen a gun up close before. My family always thought of guns as evil. No one at the Grove owned one. Out here, they are pretty much a necessity.

December 14, 1773

I shot my first deer today. I'm not sure how to feel about it. I'm excited that I will be capable of providing for my own needs, but my stomach flipped over when I saw the big buck go down. I'm not sure I'll be able to get used to killing defenseless animals. I have to keep telling myself it is for my survival.

December 20, 1773

Today, Timothy left me. He said he had to go back home for the winter. His home is Kaskaskia, Illinois. He said he would travel home by waterway. He takes the Cumberland up to the Tennessee, then turns onto the Ohio River until he finally reaches the Kaskaskia River. He asked me to come along, but I told him I wanted to stay. It will be lonely again without him. But, I don't want to leave Tennessee. You never know who might show up. Maybe I can even find my way back home.

March 15, 1774

Timothy has returned! It was so good to see him. I have had a difficult time of it since he has been gone. It was an extremely bitter winter. More snow than I can ever remember in Tennessee. Much of my time has been spent inside the cave, trying to stay warm and dry.

March 28, 1774

Timothy has been a bit somber today. He informed me that his wife has been missing for two years. She was captured by Indians. That was why he returned to Illinois. He wanted to see if she had come home. When I asked him what kind of Indians had taken his wife, he said, he didn't know for sure, but the Shawnee were causing a lot of trouble in that area lately. I have not seen any Indians since I came to the Salt Lick area.

May 9, 1774

So far, this has been a good spring for hunting and trapping. We have killed 4 bears, 5 elk, and our traps have been full of beaver, muskrat, and mink. Our days are long as we dry the meat and cure it, then stretch out the hides to tan them. Scraping the hides is hard work, but for some reason, I enjoy it.

August 7, 1774

I feel lucky to be alive. In the early morning after my birthday, I went outside to pee. I was attacked by a mountain lion. I thought I would die. Thankfully, Timothy heard the commotion and came to the rescue. He shot the cat before it could do too much damage. I ended up with several deep scratches on my stomach and arms. I was sore the next day from that heavy cat landing on me, but I'm doing ok now.

September 10, 1774

We saw a large band of Indians traveling through the Salt Lick area today. We kept our distance. I asked if Timothy knew who they were. He said they were Cherokee. He pointed out a chief to me who was near the front of the caravan. He said that he was Dragging Canoe. He told me this chief led a band of Cherokee that lived along the Chickamauga River in the south. He was the meanest, and smartest of all Cherokee. He was a fierce-looking man, even from a distance. He was tall, about six feet, and was built like an Oak tree. I hope that I never meet this man face to face.

October 30, 1774

Timothy says we will continue to trap throughout the winter. Then, he plans to travel back to Illinois in the spring to sell the furs. I will go with him this time. He said I should not only know how to trap and prepare the pelts, but I should also know about trading and selling them as well. I look forward to traveling with him on the river.

March 25, 1775

Tomorrow we leave to begin our trip to Illinois. Today we packed up all of our gear that we will take with us. The rest, we will store in the cave. We spent most of the last month building a barge to haul all of the furs we will be trading once we get to Illinois. The barge is about 20 feet long and 8 feet wide. Timothy says there will be some narrow passes for us to maneuver through, so the barge needs to be relatively narrow. I'm looking forward to a change of scenery. I've never been to Illinois.

April 5, 1775

We are now in Kaskaskia. It took us about a week to get here. Timothy says we were lucky. We've had very little rain, so the rivers were not too high. We had one close call shooting some rapids on the Ohio. I fell in at one point but was able to grab onto a rope that we were trailing behind the barge. Timothy was able to pull me back in. He said I was the biggest fish he has ever caught.

May 13, 1775

Tomorrow we will return to the salt flats. Timothy paid me after we sold the furs. I made $20. It doesn't sound like much, but $20 goes a long way around here. I bought myself a new hat. It is black and made of beaver felt and has a wide brim. It only cost me $3. I also got a nice pair of boots and some socks. They both cost me $8. Timothy told me I should get some long johns. I haven't had any underwear for over 2 years. He said they would help keep me warm in the winter and keep my buckskins from chaffing me during the summer. I went ahead and bought some for 50 cents. I still don't know if I want to wear them. They seem a little inconvenient to me.

August 4, 1775

Well, it's that time again. Today I turned nineteen. Time seems to be passing quickly now. I guess it's because I stay so busy. Some Chickasaw men passed through yesterday. They had some news about Dragging Canoe, the Chickamauga leader that we spied out here last year. He said Dragging Canoe was trying to unite the nations of all the people. By that, he didn't mean all of the people—just the Indians. Dragging Canoe made a speech in North Carolina to the people of his father, trying to convince them not to sell their lands to the white man. The Chickasaw man said he did not believe his people would join with Dragging Canoe. He said Dragging Canoe was too friendly with the Red Coats and that the Red Coats were worse than the white men settling in the east. I don't think they realize that the white men will be moving this way soon. I will not tell him either.

September 7, 1775

I haven't been feeling well. I think I have a cold. I hope it isn't the flu. I've been hanging around camp for the last two days, getting as much rest as I can.

Today I saw Red Coats traveling through the forest. I counted around fifty of them. I could see them moving down next to the Cumberland River. Near dusk they had marched out of sight, but I could see smoke rising through the trees to the north. I'm sure they had made camp for the night. I hope it is for only one night. I don't want anything to do with them.

When Timothy got back to camp, he said he had not seen them. I think it is a good thing that he didn't. I'm not too sure how friendly they would be to a Frenchman.

October 4, 1775

Timothy says we should pack up and go back north for the winter. We've got a vast store of pelts to carry with us. I don't look forward to going north for the winter, but Timothy has a cabin there for us to keep warm in instead of staying in a cave all winter. We'll leave in two days.

October 8, 1775

While floating along the Tennessee River today, we happened upon a small band of Indians. Timothy said they were Shawnee. He spoke to them in French, and one of them understood. Timothy said he asked them about his missing wife. They claimed to not know anything about her. They wanted us to give them all of our furs. They said it was payment for using their river. Timothy refused and told them it wasn't their river, it was his, and they should give us all of their furs. Timothy and I both raised our rifles at them to show we weren't going to back down. They only had bows and arrows, so they backed off and continued downriver. Timothy is a brave man, but someday I think he might get us killed.

March 17, 1776

We arrived back at the cave today. Our trip back was pretty uneventful. It's nice to be back in Tennessee. Even though we have to sleep in a cave, I prefer it to living in Illinois.

April 12, 1776

We saw another group of Red Coats come through today. We watched them from our ridge. They are a loud bunch and tend to scare away the wildlife, so we stayed close to camp today. I haven't said anything to Timothy about what is to come.

May 5, 1776

There was an accident today. Timothy got his finger caught in a bear trap as he was setting it. It was his right forefinger. Half of his finger is gone. I helped him bandage it as best I could. It was really gruesome. He is in a lot of pain but is medicating with plenty of whiskey.

July 4, 1776

It's Independence Day! The first one ever. I sure would have loved to be in Philadelphia today to see those famous men signing that iconic piece of paper. I'm sure it will be a while before news reaches us out here, but I can still celebrate in my mind.

September 5, 1776

A large group of Chickasaw came through today. They were led by a man I have seen before. His name is William Colbert. He looks to be about 30 years old. He said that he was asked to meet with General George Washington in the north. He and his people will support the fight against the British. This was the first news that Timothy had heard of the war of independence. I hope he doesn't decide to get involved. I would miss him. I have no intention of becoming involved in this war. I still have hope that I can one day find my way home.

November 11, 1776

Timothy says we will not be going to Illinois this winter. Our trapping has not been as successful of late. He wants to continue through the winter in hopes of gaining enough furs to trade in the spring. I am happy that we won't be going to Illinois this winter. I like it right here.

December 25, 1776

I have decided not to write anymore unless something very significant happens. I am running low on ink, and my book only has a few more pages in it. Next time I go to

Illinois, I will try to buy some ink and paper.

April 2, 1778

I can't believe it! I just met Daniel Boone!

Timothy and I were coming back to Tennessee from Illinois. We stopped for the night and camped along the Ohio River through Kentucky. Some men came to our camp and asked to share our fire. One of them was very tall. He turned out to be Daniel Boone. They were out on a journey to find salt for their community. He didn't look anything like Fess Parker from the TV show.

April 15, 1778

I'm glad I was able to buy more ink and paper while we were in Illinois. It's been raining continuously for the past five days, and I haven't had much to do. Guess I'll do some writing although I really don't have much to tell.

The Cumberland River is overflowing its banks right now. It's a good thing our cave is high up on this bluff. We're not likely to drown up here, but we might die of boredom.

May 5, 1778

The rain stopped about three days ago. The waters are slowly receding, and the temperature is rising. Summer isn't far off. We were able to get down off of the bluff to check our traps. Most of them were buried in mud. We found all but one of them. Timothy thinks it may have floated down the river along with the small tree it was attached to.

June 21, 1778

Today is the anniversary of Robbie's death. It was five years ago that he was killed by Indians. I still don't know how that could happen or how we ended up in this world. I sure do miss him and my mom and dad. I wonder if I'll ever see my parents again.

August 4, 1778

Well, I'm another year older. It doesn't feel like there's much to celebrate anymore. It's just another day to me.

Timothy is showing me how to make mittens out of beaver pelt. I'm not very good at it yet, but at least it gives me something to do to pass the time. Time. I'm not sure I understand the concept of time anymore.

October 10, 1778

I couldn't believe it. I woke up this morning, and it was snowing. I hope that doesn't mean we'll have a really bad winter. I don't like checking traps when it's cold. I don't like doing much of anything when it's cold.

December 26, 1779

Yesterday was Christmas. I haven't seen my family for a little over six years now. I sure do miss them!

I heard a whippoorwill last night. I thought it strange to hear one this late in the year, but I'm sure I heard it. It reminded me of when I was a boy. Robbie and I went

camping one night down by the creek that ran through the Grove. I woke up early before the sun rose. I needed to pee. When I stepped outside to find a place, I heard it.

Whip-poor-will, whip-poor-will, it sang. Robbie heard it too. That was the last time I remember ever hearing one until last night.

Timothy and I spent most of yesterday sitting on a bluff overlooking the salt flats. It was Christmas Day, and we didn't feel like working much, so we sat there and talked. Around noon, some people started to show up on the flats. Men, maybe forty of them, came from the east and settled in on the salt flats. They started cutting down trees and began constructing a stockade.

In the middle of the afternoon, boats began to arrive on the Cumberland River. There were large boats and canoes and even pirogues. I counted 30 vessels in all. Men women and children, all were arriving to build a settlement near the salt flats. Timothy decided we should go and see what they were up to.

December 29, 1779

Timothy and I have parted ways. It is sad. He has taught me so much. But, he did not like having settlers come into our area. He thinks this place is his. I can't prove it, but I'm sure he tried to burn down the fort that the people are building. I have decided to stay and help the settlers build their new town if they will let me.

March 14, 1780

The post arrived at Fort Nashborough today. I was surprised to see a letter to me from Timothy. I never expected to hear from him again since our last meeting. He said that he has gone east to fight in the revolution. He is serving under George Rogers Clark. He said he won't be back until the war has ended. He said I could have all of the traps if I wanted to continue trapping. I'm not sure if I want to anymore, but I need to do something to make money.

May 11, 1780

Many of the men have left Nashborough to fight in the war. I have managed to stay out of it. I'm sure many think ill of me in doing so, but I have stayed alive here in the frontier for nearly seven years, and I don't intend to lose my life in some war. I have found another way in which I can serve the people of Tennessee. I am hunting and trapping. I furnish meat for the women who are unable to hunt for themselves. I trade the meat for items that I might need. I also make items to trade, such as mittens, mufflers, and coats from the pelts that I trap. So far, things are going well.

May 17, 1780

Our fort was attacked by British soldiers yesterday. Four of our brave men were killed in the battle. Many others were wounded. We killed forty-three of them before they retreated. I had hoped to avoid the war by staying here at the fort rather than joining the ranks of colonial soldiers. I was wrong about that. I was not wrong about the war, however. I hope I never have to fire my rifle at another man as long as I live.

April 3, 1781

Things are growing around here. More people are moving into the area. They've got the Cherokee in an uproar. They feel like the white man is stealing their land. I guess they should have listened to Dragging Canoe when he tried to warn them. Yesterday, twenty-one men from the area looked for a bunch of the Cherokee who were raiding some of the farms. Things didn't turn out so well. It turns out that there were about two-hundred Cherokee against our small group of men. Nine of our men were killed, and many more were wounded. I try my best to stay as close to the fort as I can.

August 4, 1781

Well, I'm another year older. I turned twenty-five today. I treated myself to a canoe ride up the Cumberland River. I haven't been on the river since Timothy left. I didn't go far. I just did a little fishing and site seeing. I miss having someone to talk to like Timothy.

June 7, 1782

Twenty new families moved into the area last month. They came in from Washington County wherever that is. Somewhere in North Carolina, I think. They settled on some land just north of the Cumberland River. They are calling it Irish Station. I think I might be able to do some trading there.

October 10, 1782

I made my way over to Irish Station today. I took some furs to see if there was anything they might be willing to trade for. They had a man over there that opened a trading post. His name was Enos Clark. I traded him some beaver pelts for a new brim hat. It looks right smart with my buckskins.

March 11, 1783

I heard news today that a new road is going to be built soon. It will be the first road built in the area. No more traveling through rough trails. They say it will start at the fort and head east to a place called Mansker's Station. Stores and other buildings are going up everywhere outside of the fort now. More and more people are moving into the area.

September 7, 1783

We got word today that as of September fourth, the Treaty of Paris was signed. The war is now officially over.

April 4, 1784

The officials in charge of setting things up here have decided to set aside two hundred acres along the Cumberland River that will be sold off in one-acre lots, that will be sold for four pounds each. They are re-naming it Nashville. Four acres are going to be set aside for public buildings and a jail. I guess we are becoming civilized.

January 17, 1790

We have a new Attorney General in town. His name is Andrew Jackson. He is a man I don't want to get on the wrong side of. He scares me a bit. He is ruthless. I remember reading once that he threatened to execute Davy Crockett and his militia for trying to leave and go home after witnessing Jackson command that a whole village of Indians be wiped out. Men, women, and children were all killed. The man is full of hate.

May 5, 1793

The rain has been especially bad recently. The whole town is completely flooded. Many homes and public buildings have been destroyed. I saw a house floating down the Cumberland River today. I don't know where it might have ended up.

October 10, 1793

I met a man today that I like very much. His name is John Gordon. He has given me some work. He is originally from Virginia. He says he will soon be married, and they will be buying a farm in this area.

March 8, 1794

I met Captain Gordon's bride today. Oh yeah, he is a captain of the Tennessee Militia now. His wife's name is Delores, but she said I could call her Dolly. I think she might be good for Captain Gordon. She seems to be very skillful in business affairs and in running the household. Captain Gordon has hired me to look after their farm for him. I know a little about growing a garden, but I will depend on Miss Dolly for help with the rest of it. Captain Gordon will be traveling a lot with the militia.

June 4, 1796

As of June first, Tennessee is now officially a state. People around here are very excited about statehood. I hope they know what they're getting themselves into.

July 1, 1796

Captain Gordon was appointed to be the first Postmaster for this area. He is hiring me to be a post rider. I don't have a horse, but he said they would furnish me one. I hope I don't fall off. I've never met a horse I couldn't get thrown from.

December 12, 1796

I met a young lady today. She and her family have recently moved to the area from Virginia. I met her while delivering the post to their house. She is beautiful and seems to be just a little younger than I am. I talked to her for a little while, but her father came out and politely told me to leave while he pointed a gun at me.

April 4, 1799

I can't believe what I witnessed today. A man named Andrew Pierce was caught stealing a horse. It seems horse thieves are the worst kind of thieves around here. He was sentenced to stand chained to the public pillory outside the courthouse for one hour. He was then given thirty-nine lashes with a whip. They then cut off both of his ears and branded his cheeks. One side with an H and the other with a T. It was a gruesome sight.

October 11, 1811

Captain Gordon has fallen on hard times, it seems. Not only has he lost his job as Postmaster, but he has also incurred much debt trying to keep his plantation afloat. I am back to hunting and trapping now. He couldn't afford to hire me on the estate, and when he lost his job as Postmaster, they fired me, too. They also made me give back the horse I was using to deliver the post. They said that it belonged to the government. I didn't argue with them. I've seen what they do to horse thieves.

February 12, 1812

Captain Gordon has made a deal with one of the Chickasaw chiefs. He is William Colbert. I met him years ago when Timothy was here. The Gordons have been given some land on the Natchez Trail next to the Duck River. The chief and the captain will be partners in the ferry business. The Gordons will be farming about 650 acres there, too, and plan to open a trading post. He has hired me to run the ferry for him. He said the ferry has been there for about ten years, but there hasn't been anyone to tend to it, so it might need some repairs. It seems strange for me to be going back to the Duck River, where my life here in this world began.

June 14, 1812

We all got moved to the new farm. I'm sleeping in a tent. The Gordons built a log cabin to live in for the time being. They plan to turn it into a trading post soon. Captain Gordon was called away. General Andrew Jackson needed him as a scout for a new war we got ourselves into. He asked me if I wanted to learn to be a scout, and I said no, thank you. I'll stay here and run the ferry and help Miss Dolly with whatever I can. She and the Captain have eleven children now. Their oldest boy is John Jr. He is fifteen and helps me with the ferry sometimes.

August 7, 1812

Miss Dolly asked me to run an errand for her. She sent me across the river over to the next stand. She said it was called Sheboss. A Chickasaw man and his white wife run it. Miss Dolly wanted me to tell them that we were opening a trading post if they should need anything. She sent four jars of peaches as a gift. It took about six hours for me to get there. They let me sleep in the cabin for free. It has been a very long time since I have slept indoors. The bed was nice and soft. I slept until nearly eight o'clock. I thanked Miss Dolly for letting me run that errand for her.

March 15, 1813

Miss Dolly received a letter from the captain today. He and Chief William are fighting together against the Creek Indians down in Mississippi. The captain has bought some more land to go with the six-hundred and fifty acres they already have. They now own about fifteen hundred acres.

January 10, 1815

Miss Dolly got another letter from the captain today. He said that the war is all but over. He is in New Orleans now. The army fought a bloody battle there against the British and won. The British were running last he had seen them toward the swamps, trying to find their way to the coast. He is expecting a treaty to be signed within the month.

February 20, 1815

Captain Gordon is coming home. The British have officially surrendered and are headed back to England. You'd think they would have learned their lesson in the last war. I guess that little island of theirs just isn't big enough for them. They believe they should own the whole world.

March 1, 1815

Captain Gordon is back. It's good to see him again. The children were very excited to see him again. He and Miss Dolly are making plans to build a new house soon. He brought two new men back with him. One of them is Henry. He will be helping me with the ferry so John Jr. can run the trading post for Miss Dolly. The other man's name is Titus. He is going to be in charge of the slaves. I'm glad he didn't ask me to be in charge of them. I know having slaves is a part of life here in this time, but it just doesn't sit well with me. Some of my best friends back in California were black.

January 5, 1816

Bad news! The Gordon's youngest boy, Joshua, died last night. He was only thirteen. He was always a little sickly, but he caught the flu and just couldn't kick it. They buried him today under a big tree on the farm. Seeing that little boy being lowered into the ground made me think of Robbie. I wish I could have given Robbie a decent funeral.

August 4, 1816

Birthdays have become pretty meaningless to me, but Miss Dolly surprised me with a cake today to celebrate my birthday. I guess maybe she felt sorry for me. I'm sixty years old. My, where have the years gone.?It seems like just yesterday, I was a sixteen-year-old kid wandering around in the wilderness, trying to survive. After supper tonight, Miss Dolly and I talked alone. She saw how sad I was. I couldn't help it. I had to tell someone, and I felt I could trust her more than anyone. I told her how I came to this world. I didn't think she would believe me, but she said she had heard of such things from Indians who had come to the trading post. She thought it was just folklore, but now she says it might be true. She told me not to tell any of the Chickasaw. They would not be happy if they knew how I got here.

September 3, 1816

Captain Gordon has left again. He had to meet up with General Jackson to go fight the Seminoles down in Florida. He told Miss Dolly that he would be back from time to time and that they would start on the house he has been promising her. We'll see. The way these people run off to fight in battles, you'd think they were going to watch a football game. They get all excited, and it seems like they can't wait for another one. I'll never understand it.

October 13, 1816

I lost Henry today. We were crossing the ferry over the river with three men and their horses. One of the horses got spooked and somehow backed over Henry and pushed him into the river. I tried to throw him a rope, but he couldn't reach it. He struggled for a while, but then he went under and never came back up. He never mentioned that he couldn't swim. Henry was a good man. I will miss him.

November 2, 1816

A young man showed up at the farm today. He's been drifting across the Natchez Trail. Miss Dolly offered him a job helping me with the ferry. His name is Tom. He says he thinks he is sixteen, but he doesn't know for sure. I sure hope he knows how to swim.

March 7, 1817

Miss Dolly started construction on the new house today. She has put Titus in charge of seeing the slave men get everything just right. She and the captain converse by post about how the house is to be built. It will be a brick house. Of course, I've already seen it. But not when it was new.

December 22, 1817

A young man showed up today, leading a horse. The horse was carrying his dead friend. The clothing and the gear he had were not from the present. I think he may have come here like I did so many years ago. But how? He was as confused as I was when I first came here. I introduced him to Miss Dolly. His name is Daniel Lane. I can't wait to talk to him alone. After he went to bed, Miss Dolly asked me what I thought about him. I told her I thought he probably came here just like I did, but I don't know how either of us got here. She said she is sending him to meet David Colbert at Sheboss Stand. He might be able to help him and maybe me.

April 14, 1818

Daniel came back from Sheboss today. It was good to see him. After supper, Miss Dolly suggested I go and talk to him and tell him how I got here. I took my haversack with me and pulled out my old tie-dyed T-shirt and showed it to him. It feels so good to be able to talk to someone and not have them think I'm crazy. I have someone to share my nightmare with now. Maybe he can figure out how we can get home. I sure hope so. That is if I still have a home to go back to.

April 18, 1818

Daniel says he thinks he has discovered a way to get back home. But, he can't leave until June 21st. We talk every night now, after supper. I can't believe all the things I have missed. The world has changed so much since I left it in 1973. I hope Daniel will consider letting me go back with him.

May 1, 1818

I finally got the nerve to ask Daniel if I could go back with him. He said, yes! We are making plans on what to do once we go back through the Shimmering, as he calls it. That's the gateway that Robbie and I went through when we ended up here. I can't wait! I'm counting the days.

June 20, 1818

This will be my last entry. Daniel and I will be going home tomorrow. At least that is the plan. We still don't know for sure if it will work or not. It is just a theory that Daniel has. I told him that Robbie and I came through on June 21, 1973. He came through on December 21, 2017. So his theory is that the Shimmering only opens on the summer and winter solstice. We will test it out tomorrow. Cross your fingers. I haven't seen my home in such a long time. I can't wait to get there.

Chickasaw Glossary

The Chickasaw language is very limited in comparison to English. The words listed below are rough translations from Chickasaw to English. I am by no means an expert on any language, especially Chickasaw. This glossary is only meant to be a reference to the reader.

Ittola Chuka -
Ittola means, shimmer
Chuka meaning, door
Ittola Chuka is the Chickasaw name for The Shimmering, a portal that allows one to travel from one time to another.

Tobi Okla -
Tobi means sacred
Okla means ground
Tobi Okla is the name for the area where The Shimmering (Ittola Chuka) is located. It is an open field with burial mounds.

Ilbuk Losa -
Ilbuk means hand
Losa means black

Ilbuk Losa is the name of a group of Chickasaw who protect the sanctity of Tobi Okla. They are especially vigilant during times when Ittola Chuka is active, such as the summer and winter solstices.

Shila ah -
Shila means short
ah means day
Shila ah is the shortest day of the year, the winter solstice. It is one of the year's two days when Ittola Chuka is active.

Faloha ah -
Faloha means long
ah means day
Faloha ah is the longest day of the year, the summer solstice. It is the other day when Ittola Chuka is active.

Keyu -
Keyu means forbidden.

Nafkl -
Nafkl means brother. It is a term of endearment and honor for someone who is admired but not necessarily related.

Hallito -
Hallito is a greeting. Hello!

Shobohli ihoo -
Shobohli means cure
ihoo means, woman

Shobohli ihoo is the name given to a medicine woman or someone who practices the art of healing.

Hatuk app ala -

Hatuk means bear (typically, the name is translated as "washing bear," also known as the raccoon.

app meaning, feed

ala meaning, man

Hatuk app ala is translated as a man who feeds bears.

ABOUT THE AUTHOR

Michael L. Clark was born in Tacoma, Washington, but grew up mainly in the south. Over the years, he has worked as a farmhand, elephant handler, zookeeper, restaurant manager and owner, musician, cake artist, and rural mail carrier, all while honing his craft as a storyteller.

Clark's debut series was inspired by his many trips down the Natchez Trace. The stops along the Trail mentioned the people who once lived on the trail but gave limited information about their lives. Clark began to wonder about their stories and imagine traveling back in time to live among them and learn more. That desire sparked the idea for his first novel, The Shimmering, which has since evolved into a series of time-traveling Historical Novels.

His fourth novel, Ambush at Horse Creek, is the first of many books he calls The Young Americans series. Each story depicts a young person growing up in a historical situation. Ambush is about a teenage boy who rides for the Pony Express.

Book by This Author

The Shimmering

The Diary of Gus Childers, The Shimmering Book 2

The Prophet: The Shimmering Book 3

Ambush at Horse Creek

The Red Raven

Raven's Destiny, The Red Raven Book 2

www.ingramcontent.com/pod-product-compliance
Lightning Source LLC
Chambersburg PA
CBHW071129010826
48975CB00017B/869